Summer
at Steller's Creek

Summer
at Steller's Creek

Anne Clay Cernyar

Illustrated by
Joan M. Clay

Writers Club Press
San Jose New York Lincoln Shanghai

Summer at Steller's Creek

Writers Club Press
an imprint of iUniverse.com, Inc.

For information address:
iUniverse.com, Inc.
620 North 48th Street, Suite 201
Lincoln, NE 68504-3467
www.iuniverse.com

Cover design by John H. Clay and Joan M. Clay.

All other illustrations by Joan M. Clay.

Scripture taken from the New American Standard Bible, Copyright The Lockman Foundation 1960, 1962, 1963, 1968, 1971, 1972, 1973, 1975, 1977, 1995. Used by permission. (www.Lockman.org)

ISBN: 0-595-13729-6

Printed in the United States of America

To my sisters, Emily and Laura, with whom I share many happy memories of Frances and Molly, the dogs who inspired "Kayak" and "Lady."

Epigraph

The God who made the world and all things in it, since He is Lord of heaven and earth, does not dwell in temples made with hands; neither is He served by human hands, as though He needed anything, since He Himself gives to all life and breath and all things; and He made from one, every nation of mankind to live on all the face of the earth, having determined their appointed times, and the boundaries of their habitation, that they should seek God, if perhaps they might grope for Him and find Him, though He is not far from each one of us.

—Acts 17:24-27

Table of Contents

Preface

Dear Reader,

I'm glad you're reading *Summer at Steller's Creek*! While the characters, locations, and story are completely fictional, many of Jessica's experiences are based on my life and the lives of my friends in northwestern Montana.

Yes, there are still a few places in the Rocky Mountains where families do not yet have electricity or running water. As you will tell from the story, though, such a life can often be an adventure. Girls like Jessica find many creative ways to enjoy the outdoors and the independence that comes with living in such wild country.

The Afterword at the back of the book will further explain some of the discoveries that Jessica makes while searching for answers to her questions. I hope it will be encouraging and helpful.

God bless you.

—Anne Clay Cernyar

Foreword

Fiction is a hot commodity again. This is a generation that likes to read stories. Throughout the history of western literature, fiction often has another purpose, too—it can be a vehicle for teaching ideas. As we identify with the characters in the text, seeing how they face life and its crises, we gain insights. Sometimes these are truthful insights and sometimes they are not. Hence the need to be careful concerning what we and our families read. Some authors are so skillful that they are able to help us to both enjoy the text immensely, and grow along the way, too. The latter may even occur without our being aware of it.

This is the kind of story that you are holding in your hand. Anne Clay Cernyar is a skilled storyteller. As you read about Jessica James and her quest to train her own dogsled team, you get caught up in her adventures with her friend Penny and brother Patrick, as well as meeting Deanna Morris, who questions Jessica's faith. Along with this story, we can hear about life in a Rocky Mountain cabin apart from the normal modern necessities of life. And it's all very exciting! I immediately thought about my years living in Montana. I can imagine the scenes as they unfold.

But along the way, something else is going on, too. We learn Christian truths that further our own pursuit of Jesus Christ. Anne even brings up a few arguments for God's existence, but she does so in a manner that is not threatening. You don't have to have a college degree in philosophy. That's because good story tellers can do that sort of thing. But all the while, the reader is both stretched and given the opportunity to grow.

Enjoy yourself! *Summer at Steller's Creek* is a delightful read. Wholesomely entertaining, it keeps you reading and enjoying the story while you learn how to walk with God. I highly recommend it!

—Gary Habermas

Gary R. Habermas, Ph.D., D.D., is Distinguished Professor and Chair of the Department of Philosophy and Theology at Liberty University in Lynchburg, Virginia. Much in demand as a speaker, he is also the author of *The Historical Jesus: Ancient Evidence for the Life of Christ*, over a hundred articles, and twenty other books dealing with Christian apologetics.

Acknowledgments

Special thanks to the following family and friends for their encouragement and enthusiasm:

To my parents, John and Joan Clay, who had the courage to homeschool my sisters and me before homeschooling became as popular as it is today. Thank you for giving me the time and encouragement to pursue my interest in writing. Thank you for the beautiful illustrations that you designed for this book.

To my sisters, Emily and Laura, whose support helped make this book possible.

To the homeschoolers that I tutored on the West Kootenai whose interest in an early version of the story inspired me to keep working on it.

To Gary Habermas who graciously took time to read and comment on the philosophical ideas contained in the story.

To the English and Communications faculty at Liberty University—including Ann Wharton, Kenny Rowlette, and Olga Kronmeyer—who read all or part of this novel and gave me valuable advice.

To all who read the story, provided new perspectives, and cheered me on. Thank you!

And especially to my husband, Jeff. Marrying you was the smartest thing I've ever done.

Chapter 1: On Our Way

"Kayak, sit still!" I said, struggling to look over the head of my ten-month-old wolf-dog. "You will sit in my lap, and that's that!"

The big, black puppy, intent on putting her head out the car window, paid no attention. I shifted uncomfortably and wished we owned a bigger car. I wished Kayak were riding in the truck with my father and sixteen-year-old brother, Patrick. Most of all, I wished that I were anywhere but at a smelly gas station in the passenger seat of a hot, overloaded Toyota Corolla on a hot July day with a hot, smelly dog in my lap!

"Oh, no! Kayak!"

In one of her wild turns, Kayak whacked a tissue-wrapped bundle from the dashboard with her tail. I shoved the dog into the driver's seat, while I dove for the package and felt it anxiously. My mother's glass suncatcher had been an anniversary gift from my father, and I definitely did not want to be responsible for breaking it. Fortunately, it seemed to be okay. I wedged it into the glove compartment and corralled Kayak again as Mom returned to the car.

"Well, Jessica, it looks like we're all set!" my mother said cheerfully as she slipped into the driver's seat. "We're finally on our way."

1

I sighed. It seemed as if we had been "on our way" almost forever. In reality, we had just left the Kalispell farmhouse where I'd spent all twelve years of my life. Ahead of us lay a hundred miles of driving and a brand new life in a new town—well, not exactly in town. Our new home, way up in the Rocky Mountains, was a log cabin with no electricity or running water—unless nearby Steller's Creek counted as running water.

As our car turned the corner, I glimpsed the two-story house where my best friend, Maria, lived. Her red bike leaned against the fence, but the yard was deserted. After sad good-byes, Maria had already left for church camp—without me for the first time. We'd gone together every year since third grade.

I bit my lip as sudden tears sprang to my eyes. This was the hard part, leaving friends behind. I figured that I could handle life without electricity or running water. After all, I loved to camp, and my family had dreamed of this adventure for years. Our new home, though, lay a hundred miles from my friends and from our big homeschool group. Torch Heights, the closest town to our new cabin at Steller's Creek, was over twenty miles away. How could I ever make friends way up in the woods?

"Kayak, sit down!" Mom gently jabbed the dog with her elbow. "You can't sit in my lap while I'm driving. Jessica, please hang on to her!"

"I'm trying," I said, struggling with the dog again.

Mom pulled out onto the highway and our nightmare drive was underway. Kayak was so distracting that I didn't have time to mope. The wolf-dog persisted in standing in my lap. When I rolled down the window a crack, she struggled to put her muzzle into the wind. Her tail whipped me in the face.

In the back seat, at least my parakeet, Cheeper, was quiet. I had covered his cage with a blanket and wedged it tightly between the door and some boxes. On the other hand, my Siamese cat, Parka, yowled when we put her cage in the car, and she never stopped.

"Yaowraohhw! Yaowraohhw!"

"Can't you feed her something?" Mom asked after a while. She clutched the steering wheel so tightly that her knuckles whitened. (She hates to drive.)

"Yaowraohhw!"

"Feed Kayak?" I ducked the wet nose that turned in my direction.

"No!" Mom said. "The cat!"

"There *is* food in there," I told her.

"Yaowraohhw!"

"Maybe if you cover the cage that would help," Mom said. "Oh, fine, fine! I'll let you by! Then let's see you pass the truck."

"What?" I asked, startled.

"Not you," Mom said, maneuvering the Corolla toward the right side of the road. "That car is tailgating me way too closely."

As she spoke, a dark green Camry lunged past us and pulled up close behind our big, old Chevy truck. We couldn't see the passengers through the darkly-tinted windows, but we could hear honking as the driver urged my father to pull out of the way. Apparently our truck didn't obey soon enough. The Camry pulled out to the left and accelerated to pass, even though it was a no-passing zone.

"There's a logging truck coming!" I said.

"Good grief!" Mom stepped on the brakes.

Ahead of us, Dad stepped on his brakes. The on-coming logging truck blared its horn. Somehow the green car dodged into the right lane ahead of our truck, just in time to avoid a collision. It zipped on around the curve without stopping.

"That was really crazy!" Mom shook her head angrily. "No hurry is worth doing something foolish like that."

Just a few minutes later, the mountain of boxes that was our truck made a left turn onto a dirt road. I rolled down my window a little more and poked my head out. A single lane of cars stretched out before us with a flag-woman at the head of the line. "It's a detour," I announced.

"Oh," Mom sighed.

"And look, there's that green car just ahead of Dad," I said, struggling to see around Kayak's head. "After all that, they aren't getting anywhere any faster than we are!"

"Yaowraohhw!" my poor cat wailed from the back seat. "Yaowraohhhw!"

The new route turned out to be a long, miserable detour around a beautiful, big lake. Because of the dust and fumes, we rolled up the windows. Our air conditioner wasn't working, though, so the car got hot and smelled of exhaust and dog. Kayak panted heavily and dripped saliva on me. Mom concentrated on driving. I didn't feel much like talking, either, so we inched along in silence smack in the middle of a slow line of cars.

Although I tried not to think about it, my thoughts drifted again to my best friend, Maria, at camp. What kind of neat crafts would she learn this year? Would the speakers be interesting? How soon would I make friends at Steller's Creek? Would there even be any girls my age in teeny-tiny Torch Heights, twenty miles away? All of a sudden I was crying while Kayak tried to lick my face.

"Jessica? Are you all right?" Mom asked anxiously.

"I just miss Maria." I wiped my face and pushed away the dog's inquiring nose. "Kayak, don't."

"Sure," Mom said. She took a hand off the wheel long enough to pat me on the arm. "It'll be lonely for awhile," she said. "But you'll find friends soon, Jess. There's a good church, and we'll join the homeschool group in the fall, and Maria will come up for a few days in September."

"It won't be the same," I whispered.

"I know, but a true friend can stand the challenge of distance. And it will get easier. The Lord will help you."

I nodded.

"There are things that will make this worth it. You'll see." My mother nodded at the dog on my lap. "That's one, right there."

I managed a small smile, and my arms tightened around Kayak. Mom had a point. Ever since kindergarten, I'd longed to own a team of sled dogs and a dogsled. I'd watched a movie about a man who won a dogsled race in Alaska. Somehow, that lit a fire inside of me and I read everything that I could find about dogs and sleds.

At a rented house, though, near a trailer park, a team of dogs hadn't been workable. At least my parents didn't think so, even though I tried to persuade them that five or six big dogs couldn't cause too much trouble!

Now that we were moving to Steller's Creek, though, my parents had surprised me with Kayak—an irresistible pup with long black legs, narrow tail, and slim body. She had a saucy white mask on her face, mischievous brown eyes, alert ears, and a body that never stopped moving. Although her mother had been a black Labrador, Kayak inherited a double portion of energy and keenness from her father—a big, domesticated gray wolf. She kept my whole family on the alert because we never knew what she'd get into next.

Kayak—the first sled dog of my dream team. Comforted a little, I closed my eyes, envisioning my new pup at the head of a whole team. *The sled slipped smoothly over the deep, white snow. I stood on the runners and shouted to the lead dog who obeyed my commands instantly. After three days on the trail, the animals were tired, but willing. The other teams had quickly dropped behind, and, if we could keep up the pace, the race would be ours...*

I was jolted from my daydreams as the car finally pulled back on the highway, headed north. I rolled the window down far enough for Kayak to poke her nose into the wind. After about ten minutes, Dad and Patrick pulled the truck into a small country gas station. Mom and I parked, too, and crawled gratefully out of the car to stretch our legs.

It was then that I spotted the green Camry again, parked at the pump. A tall young man was putting gas in the tank, and two girls who looked about my age were just walking into the store—two girls so neatly dressed that they could have stepped out of a teen magazine.

I looked down at my wrinkled moving clothes, stained with ketchup from lunch, covered with dog hair, and damp from Kayak's saliva. What if the two strangers lived in Torch Heights? I couldn't let them see me like this! Just as I decided not to go inside, though, my mother tossed her change purse across the hood of the car to me.

"Here, Honey," she said. "Will you buy some cold pop and candy bars for all of us? I want to wash the windshield, and we need to hurry."

Chapter 2: Something So Great and Terrible

A bell jangled overhead as I pushed open the door and entered the Kootenai Gas N' Grocery. The cool interior felt good after the hot car ride. To my relief, I didn't see the two "magazine" girls anywhere. Heading toward the back of the store to gather the cold drinks, I hoped that I wouldn't run into them after all.

My hopes were short-lived. Just as I opened the refrigerator, I heard a pleading voice from the aisle next to mine.

"Oh, come on, Deanna," a girl said. "It won't be so bad. You really should pick out a card."

"Yeah, right!" the other girl replied bitterly. "It's all his fault we're here!"

The first girl sighed, then started in again. "If you don't buy a card here, you won't have one. And you know that Dad isn't happy about it either."

"Seems fine to me," Deanna said. "He doesn't care if the rest of us are miserable way out in the middle of nowhere."

"Well, I think he does," the other voice said. "And anyway, I don't think living at the creek is going to be that bad."

7

Neither girl said anything for a moment, then the first voice started in again, brightly, "And we already know the Ruffins' daughter—"

"Yeah," Deanna interrupted. Her voice pitched higher in a mocking imitation of someone else. "Hi! You should come to church camp with me!"

"Oh, she's a nice girl!" the first voice said angrily. "Just pick out a card, Deanna, and let's go."

"You buy one!" Deanna retorted.

As I turned around with the cold Pepsi in my arms, one of the two girls came around the corner of the shelves in such a hurry that she nearly knocked me over. She had curly brown hair, and the expression on her face was so angry that I concluded she must be Deanna. She gave me a brief glance and stomped her way out of the store.

A second later, the other girl passed me, too. She had apparently picked out the card, because she headed toward the counter to make her purchase. I hung back to select the candy bars, and also to avoid being seen again in my messy clothes. Apparently the two strangers weren't exactly the kind of friends I hoped to make! I wondered about the unknown Ruffin girl. If she went to church camp, maybe she was a Christian. Did she live in Torch Heights? If so, I might meet her sometime. I'd rather meet her than Deanna, anyway!

By the time I bought the snacks and left the store, the green Camry was gone and so was our big truck. Mom motioned me to hurry up.

"We're going to meet them at the waterfall," she said, in answer to my question. "We'll snack there."

"Waterfall?" I asked excitedly, carefully squeezing into the car so Kayak couldn't climb out. I do love waterfalls.

We drove for several minutes beside a white, tumbling river, and then pulled into a little parking space at the side of the road. Our truck had already arrived, and Lady, Patrick's gentle gray-and-white Australian shepherd, raced back to greet us. Kayak barked happily to see her.

"Here, Kitty!" My parakeet Cheeper chirped suddenly from the back seat.

"Yaowraohhhw!" Parka wailed, starting in again. "Yaowraohhhw! Yaowraohhhw!"

I hastily opened my door, allowing Kayak to burst into the fresh air and race through the weeds after Lady. Then I opened the back door and gently set Parka's cage beside the car. The Siamese cat pressed her silky, dark face against the slats, looking at me with terrified blue eyes, but I didn't dare let her out.

"It's okay," I whispered soothingly to the cat. "We'll just be here a few minutes. We'll be right back."

Pushing the cage into a shady spot, I gave the box a friendly pat and ran after my family, carrying the bag of snacks.

"Yaowraohhhw!" Parka wailed after me.

When we reached the top of the path, I saw the waterfall. Actually, "waterfall" seemed almost too lighthearted a word, like describing Mount Everest as a "small hill." This falls roared and foamed.

Huge, wet, black rocks were wedged into a narrow ravine at strange angles to each other. They looked as if they were trying to hold back the tons of clear, rushing mountain water that forced its way through, smashing into one unyielding surface after another. Some places the water slipped over the smaller rocks, dropping straight down the other side in sheets of white. Sometimes it channeled through tiny cracks, spraying out through every possible opening. Sometimes it fell for five or ten feet and then wrapped underneath itself in a boiling froth.

"Pretty grand, isn't it?" Dad shouted to be heard over the roaring. He stood near the edge, his arms folded across his chest, a smile on his broad face.

I looked again at the violent water and jagged rocks. Suddenly, I felt terrifyingly small, as if one misstep would send me tumbling into the grasp of something so great and terrible that nobody on earth could control it. Frightened, I wanted to move away from the hilltop, but the falls were so glorious I couldn't look away.

My sixteen-year-old brother, Patrick, broke the spell. "Hey!" he yelled enthusiastically. "I think I could get out to the middle if I jumped across that one spot!"

Horrified, I swung around to look at him, only to see his brown eyes laughing at the expression on my mother's face. "Just kidding, Mom!" he said.

She shook her head with a wry smile.

After a while, we moved on. It was still another hour to our new house, but the summer days were long. When we finally turned on to Steller's Creek Road, the sun had only just begun to set.

The unpaved, one-lane road was full of deep ruts. So Mom drove carefully with one side of the car in the middle of the road and the other tires balancing on the edge. Pines, firs, and aspen trees crowded in on either side, and twice we saw whitetail deer bounding away. Once a dark blue bird swooped across the road in front of us and disappeared into the trees.

"There goes a Steller's jay," Mom said.

"Is that what Steller's Creek is named after?"

"Probably."

After a mile, we passed a big meadow. A blue trailer was parked under trees at one end, but I didn't see anybody around.

Plunging back into the forest, we wound around a few more corners and crossed Steller's Creek—a wide, clear stream running swiftly over brown and gray stones. Then we broke into another clearing and saw a log cabin with a long, narrow porch running across the front of it. There was a big wooden step exactly in the middle of the porch, right in front of the wide door. Large windows on either side of the door reflected the last of the sunlight that spilled over the mountain peaks. My mother stopped the car in front of the house, and we piled out of the vehicles and rushed to unpack essentials before it grew dark. Since the house had no electricity, we certainly didn't have a yard light!

Eagerly I headed for the cabin and shoved open the front door. Piles of boxes lined the walls, and Kayak and Lady pushed past me and sniffed about in the dark corners.

The downstairs was divided into four rooms. The biggest, a combination living room and kitchen, stretched all the way across the front of the house. Ahead of me, a hallway divided my parents' room to the left from the washroom and office to the right. Above me, instead of a second floor, two bedroom lofts faced each other. They were connected on one end by a small walkway. Eventually, Dad planned to build a staircase, but for now a ladder ran from the walkway down into the living room. Carrying some of my blankets, I climbed awkwardly to my loft.

It was actually quite large, since it ran the width of the house. In the middle of the room, I could stand up straight. The roof sloped away on either side until it almost touched the floor, making the room cozy. I hoped we could build cupboards along the walls where I couldn't stand up.

Although the room was rather dark, I found the bed and put my blankets down. (My father and Patrick had set up the frame the week before.) Then I crawled onto the mattress, propped my elbows on the windowsill, and looked down through the gray twilight at the action in the front yard.

My mother emerged from the car with another box. She nearly tripped over Kayak as she stepped onto the porch below me, and the wolf-dog sprang out of the way with agile alarm.

My father bent over something at the edge of the driveway. When a sudden burst of light illuminated his face, I realized he had lit a gasoline lantern. We'd always had lanterns for camping, but now we would use them in our house. When Dad picked up the light, it swung back and forth slightly, causing strange shadows to dash away in all directions. I could hear its loud hissing as Dad came inside.

The door banged a second time, and I heard something land on the floor with a thump. "Jessica?" Patrick shouted. "What do you want me to do with your cat?"

"Yaowraohhhw!"

We spent the rest of the evening unloading by flashlight and lantern. We fixed a cold dinner, sitting on the living room floor. After that, I made my bed in the funny half-dark of candlelight and tried to comfort Parka—a frightened and irritable ball of cat fur who persisted in hiding under my bed.

Eventually, Dad turned off the lantern. We all headed off to bed, leaving the two dogs to sleep on the living room floor.

I crept under my covers, shivering from the chill of the night mountain air, and lay awake for a long time. I thought about Maria, our drive to Steller's Creek, and the glorious waterfall. I wondered about Deanna and the other girl. It suddenly occurred to me that "the creek" where they lived might mean Steller's Creek. I hoped not! I sure didn't want to be mocked for going to church, like Deanna had mocked the mysterious Ruffins.

Then I pushed the unpleasant thoughts from my mind. They probably didn't live anywhere close. After years of dreaming and planning for our own home in the mountains, we had finally arrived at Steller's Creek. Tomorrow I would really explore!

Chapter 3: The Aspen Tunnel

Whack! Thunk!

My eyes flew open at the unexpected sound. Gazing at the peaked roof above me, I blinked in confusion. Where was I?

Whump! Crack!

Suddenly the events of the previous day flooded over me. I sat up eagerly in bed, and turned to prop my elbows on the windowsill. Down below me, Patrick wielded a huge axe. He swung it up high and brought it down on a chunk of firewood with a ferocious whack. Little splinters flew as the chunk split in half. My brother threw the two pieces to one side and reached for another log. He'd split a lot of wood even in Kalispell, where we used both wood and electric heat. Now, though, since we just had wood stoves, he and my father faced even more work.

Lady, Patrick's Australian shepherd, calmly watched everything from the shade of the trees, simply content to be near her beloved master. Kayak the wolf-dog appeared around the corner of the house. Intently sniffing along the ground, as if trailing something, she disappeared around the other corner.

Overhead, the hot July sky stretched from the jagged edge of the mountain peaks into infinity. I counted six different shades of blue sky and four different shades of gray and white clouds. The sun shone. The trees were green—a wonderful day to explore!

13

I scrambled out of bed and quickly changed into a pair of denim shorts and a blue shirt. After pulling my straight brown hair into a long ponytail, I climbed down the ladder with my black leather sandals swinging from my hand. My mother was unpacking books in the living room, putting them in order on the oak bookshelves.

"Hi!" I greeted her happily, plopping onto the couch to fasten my sandals.

"Good morning." Mom smiled at me as she added a copy of *Little House on the Prairie* to the top shelf. She looked at it a moment, then transferred it to another spot. "The rest of the series has got to be here somewhere…How did you sleep?"

"Good! May I go exploring?"

"I guess so," Mom replied. "I'll need your help to unpack after awhile, though. Eat something first. There's cereal in the box beside the cookstove, and the milk is in the creek."

"Okay." I hopped up and rummaged through the box beside the kitchen stove. Fortunately, the cereal was on top. As I dug farther, I discovered a bowl and spoon among other miscellaneous items. Then I skipped through the front door and danced toward Steller's Creek to find the milk. In Kalispell, we used a regular refrigerator, of course. Keeping things cold in the creek was new.

It was one of those perfect days, not too hot and not too cold. A faint breeze tossed a wisp of hair across my face, and I blew it back. Kayak seemed to be as joyful as I felt. She scampered around the corner of the cabin and blundered ahead of me. Splashing into the creek, she scooped up mouthfuls of water as she waded along the edge.

Someone had built a small stone wall in the creek, allowing water to flow past the food containers without washing them away. The gallon of milk had been propped upright between three more big rocks so the current wouldn't knock it over. A board covered the top of the jug.

"That must be to keep you from licking the lid," I observed to Kayak. She looked interested. "Nope, this isn't for you!" I tossed the board on the ground and carried the milk to the house.

Mom still knelt among the stacks of books. There must have been at least six big boxes full in the living room alone. My father collects books on how to build everything from cabins to cars. He also enjoys history and theology. (He taught theology at a college in Kalispell, but planned to take a sabbatical and write a book during our first year at Steller's Creek.) Mom collects old, hardcover classics and old children's stories with beautiful color illustrations. (Actually, I don't mean that the children are old—the books are.)

Both my parents also love adventure stories. Since Patrick and I are homeschooled, we spend a lot of family time reading aloud, especially in the winter. We've sailed the seas with *Kon-Tiki*, explored a deserted island with *Robinson Crusoe*, and crossed the prairies with Laura Ingalls Wilder. We spent one winter climbing Mount Everest, traveling across icy Alaska with poems by Robert Service, and exploring Antarctica. Another year took us back in history to the tumultuous times of *Lorna Doone*, *Kidnapped*, and *Treasure Island*. Of course, we've traveled to Narnia with Peter, Susan, Lucy, and Edmund. None of us could imagine a life without books—which explains why we own a humungous collection!

"Where are you going to put them all?" I added sugar to my cereal. Parka purred around my ankles, so I poured her some milk in one of our cereal bowls.

My mother observed me seriously. "Why don't you use that old plastic dish instead?"

Startled, I looked at my cat, contentedly lapping out of Mom's blue and white china. "Oh, I'm sorry."

"Look out!" The front door banged open. My father staggered in backward, holding up one end of another bookshelf. Patrick struggled with the other end, trying to tip it sideways to get through the door.

"Look out!" I echoed in alarm as Dad stepped into the bowl of milk. It flipped upside down. Parka sped away in a huff, her tail puffy.

"What was that?" Dad sounded surprised, but he was too busy trying to get the bookshelf through the door to look at what he'd stepped on. "Here, Patrick, push that corner up."

Glad the bowl had not cracked, I rescued it and tucked it safely out of the way before pouring Parka another breakfast. This time I used an orange, plastic dish.

Dad and Patrick shoved the big bookshelf against the living room wall, and then stood back to admire the job. "That should work!" My brother said with satisfaction, just as Mom asked, "Don't you think we should nail it to the logs?"

They decided they should. Dad was pounding cheerfully away with the hammer by the time I finished eating and slipped out the door into the sunshine. Kayak bounced to meet me.

Together we walked around the cabin toward the forest. The ground made a nice little meadow around the house, but it rose steeply at the edge of the trees. I'd explored the property once before, but that had been with the real estate agent and my mother insisted that I stay in sight of the house. Now, though, we actually owned the property!

When I reached the edge of the trees, I discovered a faint path that led up to another small clearing, dotted with big, old rotting stumps. When we were younger, Maria and I loved to hollow out parts of stumps to make caves for our dolls. These would have been perfect. I found one giant log all covered with moss—a wonderful spot to sit and read a Nancy Drew mystery.

At the other side of the clearing stood a whole cluster of young aspen trees, all about my height, with white trunks and round green leaves. They were so thick on the tops that I got down on my hands and knees to crawl through. When I did, I found another path.

It was a crawl-path, really, or a tunnel. The leaves and branches formed the roof overhead, leaving just enough room for me to sit upright if I wanted to. The path twisted around like a maze, so I just kept crawling to see where it led. Kayak wiggled past me and pushed ahead. It was just her size. After a minute or two, the trees thinned out. We emerged into a patch of tall pines, and I stood up and looked around.

I had crawled right into someone else's place. To my right, a tire swing hung from a crossbeam between two tall pines. There was a bare area underneath the swing from somebody's feet scuffing back and forth across the ground. I took a couple steps forward.

"Hello?" I said, uncertainly. "Is anyone here?"

Nothing stirred. Nearby, I noticed a little white picnic table snuggled between four trees and dusted with dead pine needles. Behind it, a ladder leaned against one of the pines. Looking up, I spotted a sturdy, wooden treehouse, just a little higher than my father's head.

"It must have belonged to the other people!" I told Kayak hopefully. The excitement bubbled up inside of me. This secret place was on our new land!

Leaving my wolf-dog to explore by herself, I reached for the first rung and scrambled up to investigate the treehouse. A trap door pushed right open, so I poked my head inside.

To my surprise, the room was furnished. Sunlight spilled in from small windows on each side. A collection of books nestled in a little white bookshelf against the far end. In the middle lay a red, beanbag chair—the kind you can squish down in. A tan teddy bear in a blue dress sprawled on a crate nearby, underneath a small picture of two children on a bridge with an angel hovering over them.

A clear bird feeder, full of seeds, hung outside the window right where someone could watch the birds eat. I wondered briefly if Steller's jays ever came after the seeds. To me, they are the most beautiful birds in the world.

Eagerly I pulled myself up. The books turned out to be a bird guide and stories—a Hardy Boys mystery, *Little Women*, and some unfamiliar ones. They looked well-used, and the corners of the covers were bent.

When I picked one up, out fell a handmade, paper bookmark with a name printed on it.

"Penny," I read aloud, turning the bookmark over in my hand. Wide-eyed I looked around. Who was Penny? Why had she left all these nice things behind?

Just then I heard a distant whistle from the direction of our cabin. It sounded like my mother's "Jessica, come home!" whistle, so I scrambled hastily down the ladder. With Kayak at my heels, I crawled back through the secret tunnel. Would Dad know who built the treehouse? Could it be mine?

Chapter 4: Penny

I raced down the hill and rounded the corner of the house to find my mother standing on the porch, a small yellow whistle in her hand. She looked relieved when she saw me.

"There you are," she said cheerfully. "I just wondered where you were."

"Mom!" I exclaimed. "I've only been gone half an hour!" It always amazes me how much Mom worries.

She laughed. "Don't go too far until you know your way around. It would be easy to get lost in these woods."

I wondered how I could know my way around without going there first, but I just nodded and followed her into the house. It was time to help, anyway.

"What do you want me to do?" I offered.

The big room was already starting to look like home. Mom had rescued her stained-glass suncatcher from the car, and it hung in the kitchen window, reflecting a shaft of colored light onto the metal surface of the cream-and-green cookstove. Most of the books had appeared on the new bookshelves.

Heaps of boxes decorated the kitchen floor, and more lined the walls. Some were neatly labeled "dishes" or "food." In our last rush of packing, though, many of them had simply been marked "miscellaneous." It looked as if we could both be busy for a long, long time.

"I'm not sure where everything is," my mother said wryly. "Why don't you just start on this side and put things in the cupboards? I'll finish cleaning the lamps and then give you a hand."

In addition to gasoline lanterns, we had two glass lamps that burned scented kerosene. They got dirty rather quickly, though, with soot from their smoking wicks. Every few days, Mom would take the glass globes off and gently wipe them clean. It was a messy job, and so I was glad she hadn't asked me to do it!

I tackled the unpacking, instead. I found a couple of boxes containing plates and cups. That kept me busy for several minutes, but not too busy to tell Mom all about the mysterious treehouse.

"Is it on our property?" I eagerly concluded my description.

"I doubt it." Mom hesitated, and I felt my shoulders slump in disappointment. "Did you say it's past that grove of little aspens on top of the hill?"

I nodded. She shook her head. "The property line runs just this side of those trees. You should be able to see little red flags marking the edge."

Come to think of it, I had noticed a few reddish-orange plastic ribbons tied to branches on the older trees. I sighed, disappointed.

"Hey, Mom, here are your geese." Patrick shoved the kitchen door shut behind him and deposited another large brown carton onto the couch. "They were mixed in with the tools in the shop."

"Now how did they get there?" Mom washed the soot from her hands and then anxiously opened the box flaps.

My mom is goose-crazy. She just loves to collect dishes or statues or anything with geese on them. Once our relatives found out that she likes geese, they started buying them for her birthday and Christmas. We use dishes with little white geese all around the edge attached together by a blue dotted line. We have pot holders—about ten of them—with geese wearing bows around their necks. Some sport cheery red bows for Christmas; others wear blue. One aunt even sent us a

Halloween goose that resembled a witch on a broomstick. My mother didn't keep it, though, since we don't celebrate Halloween.

Now she carefully unrolled a set of little glass geese, checking to make sure they hadn't broken their tiny, glass necks. She had each little figure all wrapped up in tissue paper.

"Does it look as if someone is still using the treehouse?" she asked, resuming our conversation.

"What treehouse?" Patrick plopped down onto the couch and put his arms behind his head. I told him what I had found.

"Someone might be using it," I finished. "It's a girl's treehouse, and she likes birds."

"How do you know that?" Patrick teased, propping his big, booted feet on a nearby carton. "What's the difference between a girl's tree-house and a boy's treehouse?"

"I can tell!" I insisted, giving the table an emphatic thump with my fist. "There's a bird feeder hanging right outside the window, and it's full of seeds. One of the books on the shelf is a bird book with lots of pictures."

"That doesn't mean she likes birds," Patrick said. "Maybe she has a cat and the cat likes to watch the birds. And maybe it isn't a girl at all."

I glared at him. "I know she's a girl," I said. "Some of those books were girls' books, and there was a teddy bear wearing a dress. Besides, a bookmark said 'Penny' on it. Do you know any boys named Penny?"

"Well," my mother intervened strategically, "There's another cabin up the road a little farther. Maybe the treehouse belongs to one of their kids. Dad and I drove past there earlier in the summer, but no one was home."

A new thought occurred to me, and I perked up. "Maybe she'll be the same age as I am!"

"Probably not," Patrick said, annoyingly. "And remember, you were trespassing."

"I was not!" I said, just as another thought occurred to me. What if the treehouse belonged to Deanna and her sister? Could the dark-haired girl be named Penny? As quickly as the thought crossed my mind, I dismissed the idea. Surely the two fashionable teenagers wouldn't hang out in a treehouse watching birds! I just couldn't picture it.

"Hey, Patrick?" Dad looked in the kitchen window, and tapped his fingers on the glass. "I found what you were looking for. Where do you want it?"

"What I was looking—Oh, yeah!" Patrick sprang to his feet.

"What were you looking for?" I wanted to know.

"Just my junk, that's all," Patrick said, hastily closing the door behind him. I jumped up, curious about my father's vague question and puzzled by my brother's mysterious look.

"It sure would be nice if they do have a daughter your age." Mom picked up the conversation so suddenly that I stopped en route to the door and looked back in surprise. She calmly unwrapped yet another goose. "But if not, maybe you'll meet some other girls in the home-school group. Have you thought about any extra subjects that you want this fall? We'll need to order the new books soon."

As a matter of fact, I wanted to study Spanish, but hadn't had a chance to mention that yet. Distracted from my pursuit of Patrick, I turned back to join my mother. We spent the rest of the hour chatting about plans for the school year and a couple new textbooks I wanted. One great thing about homeschooling is that I get to try some new subjects every year. Now, if only I could skip a few that I don't like!

As it turned out, I didn't wait too long to find out who really did own the little treehouse. Later that afternoon, I was in the loft unrolling my wolf poster with the moon in the background when I heard the rumbling of a car. Peeking out my window, I saw a blue Suburban—big enough for sixteen people, it seemed—pull into our driveway.

A short man with black hair hopped energetically out of the driver's side to greet Dad and Patrick on the porch. A tall blond lady and a girl hopped out of the other side. The girl looked shorter than I. She wore a pink baseball cap on backward, a pair of overall shorts, and a pink

T-shirt. She marched right up to my mother, who had just come outside, and started talking. Mom listened a moment, nodded, and then gestured towards the house.

With a wave back at her mother, the stranger skipped up the steps and through our front door, banging it behind her. To my astonishment, I realized she must be looking for me, but I was too shy to move.

"Jessica?" a merry voice sang out. "Where are you?"

"Up here!" I yelled back, swinging my feet off the bed. I moved toward the edge of the loft. "Come on up!"

Feet scuffled up the ladder, and the stranger appeared at my door. We looked at each other in silence for a moment. The girl had wide, friendly, brown eyes and a smattering of freckles sprinkled across her pug nose. Her short, fluffy brown hair just reached to her shoulders, and she wore straight bangs in the front.

"Hi!" she said after a pause. "I'm Penny!"

Chapter 5: I've Never Seen Any

"Can I come in?" Penny asked happily. "Are you really going to stay here? Is that your dog outside?"

I moved away from the door, and she marched cheerfully into my room, her brown hair bobbing on her shoulders. When she discovered that we had moved to Steller's Creek to live, she bubbled over with enthusiasm. "You're staying! I can't believe it! Finally, somebody my age! What do you like to do?"

Within minutes, I found myself outside. Penny and I explored all around my house and waded in the creek. She just loved Kayak and Lady, so we played with Kayak in the water for a long time. (Lady didn't like water, so she just barked anxiously from the bank.) Then Penny even helped me clean out Cheeper's bird cage and put in fresh paper and seed. All the while she chattered about things we could do before school started again. I soon decided that life at Steller's Creek could never be dull with Penny Ruffin around!

Penny was eleven, almost two years younger than I. An only child, she lived about half a mile from our house. Her treehouse stood almost halfway between our homes, and the things that I had guessed about her were right. She absolutely loved birds. As a matter of fact, I discovered just how much when I pedaled my red bicycle up the dirt road to the Ruffins' cabin the next day.

Just as I leaned the bike against the fence in the front yard, a huge, black bird swooped off the roof of the house and flew at my face. I screamed and ducked. The bird missed me, sailing lazily past and landing on a fence post.

"Don't worry about the crow!" Penny's father was on the front porch, sharpening his chain saw. He smiled to reassure me. "He's Penny's pet. He won't hurt you."

"Pet?" I asked, looking at the bird. He tipped his head, took several sideways steps along the top rail of the fence, peered at me with a bright eye, and then started beaking about in his feathers as though he had no further interest.

Suddenly Penny appeared on the porch. "Hi!" she yelled. "Come on in, Jess! We're making doll hats!"

"Hi!" I said. "I didn't know you had a crow."

"Oh, did you see him?" Penny bubbled. "His name is St. Peter. I've had him since he was a baby."

"He still *is* a baby," her father laughed. "A big, hungry baby."

Penny stepped over to the bird and put her fist gently against the soft feathers on the front of his chest. With an indistinct mutter, St. Peter put one clawed foot on her hand and then the other foot. Then he marched up Penny's arm and stood on her shoulder, nibbling her ear with his beak.

"Ouch!" Penny said. "Stop it!"

"Where'd you get him?" I put out a tentative finger to touch St. Peter's shiny black feathers. The crow cocked his head and looked at me.

"He fell out of a nest," Penny said. "Dad picked him up and brought him home, and we kept him in a cage until he was big enough to fly. We fed him dog food when he was little—canned dog food. He'd jump up and down in his cage and caw whenever he saw us. But now you're loose, aren't you, Pal?" She addressed her last comment to the bird.

"Wow!" I couldn't believe it—a real, live, adopted wild animal. I'd always wanted some kind of wild pet, like a fawn or a baby raccoon. I once read a story about a boy who had a pet raccoon that opened screen doors with its little hands.

"Penny?" Her mother stuck her head out the cabin door. "I'm taking the hats out of the oven!"

"Oh, yes!" Penny pushed a protesting St. Peter off her shoulder and rushed inside. "Come on!"

Wondering how a person could take doll hats out of the oven, I followed. Unlike our cabin, Penny's house was divided into rooms downstairs and I couldn't see the log walls. They were covered over with wallpapered boards. The kitchen, the first room we entered, had cheery yellow-flowered wallpaper and lots of green plants along the sill of the wide window that looked over the front yard.

Penny's mom appeared rather hot and tired in her blue jeans and green blouse, but she smiled at me. "Hello, Jessica," she said, scooping up a set of hot mitts from the kitchen counter. "You're just in time to see Penny's hats."

She opened the door of the oven and pulled out a cookie sheet. On the sheet were eight white foam cups that had melted down on the edges so that the middles stuck up. They did look just like little white hats.

"See," Penny explained, pointing to the table where an assortment of the misshapen cups lay scattered about. "We melt them and then decorate them for doll hats. Mom will use them for table decorations at the nursing home."

"I work in a nursing home part-time," Mrs. Ruffin explained to me, rapidly removing the cups from the cookie sheet. "I plan games and activities for the residents there."

I nodded. Penny had told me that she sometimes went to work with her mom. She described the older people that she visited, and how they liked to hear her read to them. I had a hard time imagining Penny sitting still long enough to read. But, it sounded as if she went a lot—especially for the parties!

Many of the little hats had been finished already, and they were really cute. Penny and her mother had tied narrow ribbons around the brims and glued on little flowers and beads. Some even sprouted tiny feathers, like parakeet feathers.

"Actually, these are decorations for a fashion show that the home is having," Mrs. Ruffin explained. "We give shows about four times a year. The one next week has the theme 'The Good Old Days.' The hats are party favors to put by the plates."

"Am I coming?" Penny wanted to know.

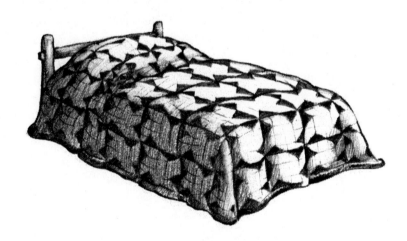

"I don't know, we'll see," her mother said. "I think Dad's working that night, so you may have to come with me."

"I think you should make sunbonnets next time," Penny proposed, running a strip of red ribbon through her fingers. "Ones like Grandma made for me."

"That's an idea," her mother said. "I'd say that would be a big job. Why don't you show Jessica your room? We'll finish these up later."

"Sure!" Penny led the way upstairs to her cheerful, bright bedroom. A pretty quilt with a red pinwheel design on it enveloped the bed. It matched the wide red ribbons that tied back the fluffy white curtains at the windows. A red and white braided rug was rolled up and standing on end in one corner, with a cowboy teddy bear sitting on top of it. Two big orange rugs shaped like bare feet lay beside the bed. They clashed so obviously with the rest of the decor that I suspected Penny's mom liked the red and white, but Penny added the orange rugs.

A stack of books lay in another corner. Penny had apparently removed them from their appointed place because the white, painted bookshelf was filled with doll furniture, made to look like a house. A ladder, made of cardboard from a cereal box, was taped to the second floor of the "house." There didn't seem to be any dolls anywhere inside, though.

"Yes!" Penny had been rummaging in a cedar chest at the foot of her bed. She gleefully pulled out a blue and white sunbonnet. "Here it is!" She threw her baseball cap on the bed, and pulled her sunbonnet on instead, tying the white ribbons under her chin. "Grandma made it for me to wear in the parade last year."

"It's pretty!" I admired. "Where are your dolls for the dollhouse?"

"Outside," my new friend explained, leaving me to wonder why. "Oh, and guess what?"

She dove back into the chest and emerged with what looked like two gray blocks with antennas. "We can use my walkie-talkies!"

"Really? Walkie-talkies?"

"My uncle gave them to me for Christmas, but I never had anybody to call before. Now we can each use one."

Eagerly we plopped onto the bed, and Penny twisted the dial on one. Nothing happened.

"Huh." Penny shook it, then tried the other. The dial clicked, but otherwise the little radio was silent. Disappointment flooded her face. "I guess the batteries are dead. Dad'll have to get some more."

"It would be neat," I said, twiddling with the other dial.

Penny sighed, but a second later she bounced up again. "Oh, you've got to see this!"

She pulled aside her pinwheel quilt and knelt down to look under the bed, so I got down on my knees, too. I saw a wooden floor, bare except for dust and some wadded-up balls of aluminum foil. I looked at my new friend.

"Those are for the packrats," she said confidentially.

"What's a packrat?" I shuddered without meaning to. I hated rats! We didn't have any at our house in Kalispell, fortunately, but I saw them in the pet shops. I hoped they weren't common at Steller's Creek.

"They're a special kind of rat that borrows things," Penny whispered back. "They like shiny stuff. So, when they take something, like these balls, they always trade you something else—something better, maybe a watch."

"Do you have them in your house?" I asked.

"I've never seen any," Penny said. "But that doesn't mean there aren't any."

Off and on all afternoon Penny regaled me with stories about packrats, the elusive, bushy-tailed creatures of the woods that no one ever saw during the summer. She explained that they lived outside when the weather was warm, but liked to move inside during the winter when the temperature dropped below freezing. She told me about their nests—big bundles of black moss and other collected things, including wads of paper and old socks. Most enthusiastically of all, Penny explained how the packrats love to trade things.

"Whenever they take one thing, they leave something else," she said to me as we watched birds from her treehouse. "Something they got somewhere else. It would be so neat to find a gold watch."

I started to see a problem. "But if they leave you a watch," I puzzled, "wouldn't they have to steal it from somebody else?"

Penny frowned at this idea. Apparently she hadn't thought of that before. Then her face brightened. "Maybe they'll find an antique," she said, as though that solved everything.

Chapter 6: Unwelcome Neighbors

In the days that followed, Penny and I found all kinds of things to do together. We scouted for wildflowers, identified wild birds, and played wild games in the creek with Kayak. Penny loved to build little boats for her tiny dolls, and we sent them on fearful adventures through the small rapids near our cabin. We spent hours in the treehouse, laughing and chattering and making up more plans. Her friendship made so much difference in the way I felt about Steller's Creek. Although I still missed Maria, I began to wonder why in the world I'd wanted to stay in Kalispell!

If Penny had been our only neighbor, I would have been content. Unfortunately, though, the Ruffins weren't our only neighbors. The other family on Steller's Creek Road were the Morrises, Penny told me. They had two daughters, Dixie and Deanna. From Penny's description, I was almost positive that they were the teenagers that I'd seen at the Kootenai Gas N' Grocery during our move.

"We'll need to go down and introduce you," Mom said brightly, when she heard the news.

I wasn't at all sure that I wanted to meet them, but I didn't have any choice. Just one week later, I was sitting on the front steps of our cabin watching Dad fix an old radio when the dark green Camry emerged from the trees and stopped at the house. A tall blond man and a dark-haired lady got out, followed by the two girls. The couple introduced themselves as Ryland and Patricia Morris. They had moved to Steller's Creek from Missoula a few weeks earlier and were just venturing out to meet their neighbors.

"We live down the road where the blue trailer is parked," Mr. Morris explained. A tall, stringy-looking man, he glanced around the porch and yard as if looking for something. "You've got a nice piece of property here."

Mrs. Morris had long dark hair. Her eyebrows looked as if they had been shaved off and then drawn on again with pencil. Her deep purple eye shadow matched her fingernail polish and her big, dangly earrings. She gushed as she introduced herself to Mom. "We are so glad to have you all here. This place is just adorable, and it will be wonderful to have more neighbors!"

Then she turned to me. "These are our girls, Dixie and Deanna," she continued, motioning to the pair behind her. "How old are you, Dear?"

"I'll be thirteen in two weeks," I said proudly.

"Thirteen?" The fake eyebrows went up slightly in surprise. "Oh my, you look so much younger!"

Before I could reply, Mrs. Morris patted me on the arm. "But, Dear, how lucky! We all wish we looked younger."

I didn't think that looking younger was a big deal for my mom. I almost said so, but managed to stop myself just in time. My mother put an arm around my shoulders and gave me a slight squeeze.

Mrs. Morris fussed on. "You're Deanna's age! She's thirteen and Dixie is fifteen. Girls, isn't this just wonderful?"

Dixie smiled at me, but Deanna, the younger one, looked just as cross as she had in the grocery store. The look she gave me was almost a glare, and I wondered anxiously why she disliked me already. They were both taller than I, wore lots of make-up, and looked like models for a clothing ad. Suddenly I wished that my mom would let me wear make-up, too—or at least that I had had enough time to wash my muddy feet! I'd been playing in the creek with Kayak, and my clothes were speckled with mud, too.

"Do you have time for a cup of coffee?" Mom smiled at Mrs. Morris and turned to the girls. "Or lemonade?"

The offer was accepted immediately, and we all moved toward the front door—everyone except Patrick, that is. As soon as he had been properly introduced and given everyone his typical, shy smile, he vanished around the cabin in the direction of his woodworking shop.

To my alarm, I realized that I would have to entertain Dixie and Deanna all by myself. Although most of his buddies in Kalispell either dated or wanted to date, Patrick frequently declared that girls were "a bother." So far, he seemed content to hike, fish, build things, and tinker around under the hoods of our cars—although some of the girls at our old church tried desperate measures to get his attention.

"Why don't you show the girls your room?" my mother suggested to me as the adults sat down around the kitchen table. "I'll have the lemonade ready in a few minutes."

I looked at the two strangers. "Would you like to come up?"

Dark-haired Dixie smiled again. "Sure!"

Obligingly, I led the way up the ladder. When we entered my door, I noticed that I'd left my dirty clothes in a pile on the floor the night before. Embarrassed, I tried to kick them under the bed, hoping my company didn't notice.

"What a beautiful cat!" Dixie exclaimed, spying Parka curled comfortably on the quilt. "Look, Deanna, a Siamese!"

"Yeah," Deanna muttered, plopping down on the bed.

Dixie ignored the lack of enthusiasm as she petted Parka. The cat stretched and purred, the picture of dignity without a hair out of place.

"Is she yours?" Dixie asked, posing casually on the bed.

"Yes," I said. "Do you have cats?"

"Just one," Dixie said. "I wish we had more. I love animals. When did you move in?"

"Last week. We used to live in Kalispell." I explained how my parents had purchased the house just two months earlier.

"We moved here a month ago," Dixie said. "We used to come to Steller's Creek just for vacations, but my dad sells real estate in Torch Heights now, so we moved."

"Where will you go to school?" Deanna interjected suddenly.

"I'm homeschooled." I watched closely for her reaction. "How about you?"

"Oh!" Deanna sounded surprised. "I'm going to Torch Heights Junior High, but Dixie has to take the bus to McCleod."

"That's a long trip." I tried to recall where McCleod was. I thought we passed it on the way from Kalispell.

"It must be neat to homeschool," Dixie said politely. "I'll be riding that old bus for over an hour one way."

"I think it'd be boring to stay home all the time," Deanna said bluntly. She looked me straight in the eye, and I had the sudden impression that she wanted to make me cry or something. Well, she was out of luck.

"I like homeschooling," I retorted, lifting my chin and staring straight back at her.

"Deanna," Dixie said in a warning tone.

To my relief, my mother called us down for lemonade right at that moment. We took the tall glasses outside.

"Where'd your brother go?" Dixie asked.

"Oh, he's working on something out back," I said with a shrug.

"Oo, Dixie!" Deanna half-whispered in a teasing tone. "Got your eye on somebody? What about Jarod?"

Dixie tossed her black curls a bit. "I'm just asking!" she said. "How old is your brother?"

"Sixteen," I replied, uncomfortable. I didn't think Patrick would have appreciated the conversation. I almost told them that he didn't like girls and wanted to be a single missionary in the middle of the Amazon jungle. Fortunately, I caught myself just in time. It *was* true, but I didn't think Patrick would want me to explain.

We took our lemonade down to the water and perched on the bank, watching the gentle ripples. Lady came over then, wagging her fluffy gray tail and holding her plastic green frog in her mouth.

"What a cute dog!" Dixie exclaimed. "Is she yours?"

"No, she's Patrick's," I said. "She wants you to throw the frog. Here, Lady, drop it."

Rather reluctantly, Lady dropped the frog. Dixie scooped it up. Immediately, Lady froze, her eyes on Dixie's hand. Before I could stop her, Dixie enthusiastically swung her arm and the toy flew in a graceful arc, splashed into the middle of the stream, and bobbed away.

Barking hysterically, the Australian shepherd ran along the bank. As the frog picked up speed in the current, Lady waded out, stopping unhappily when the water covered her dainty white forepaws up to her chest. I knew I'd have to rescue the frog.

"Won't she get it?" Dixie asked in panic.

"I don't think so," I said.

"Way to go, Dix," her sister chided in a know-it-all fashion.

I ran downstream and managed to get ahead of the toy. In a spot where the creek widened and the water was a bit shallower, I splashed out, sandals and all, and managed to grab the thing as it floated by.

Lady, Dixie, and Deanna all waited for me on the bank, various expressions of relief, dismay, and aloofness on their faces. Lady took the frog and shook herself dry, spraying us all with drops of water. Then she stood in front of Dixie, wagged her tail, and dropped her toy with a hopeful look. Even Deanna laughed at that.

"Okay." Dixie scooped up the wet toy. "You're going to let me try again? I'll keep it out of the water this time!"

After we entertained the dog for awhile, I took the girls around to introduce them to Kayak, tied by her doghouse at the edge of the trees.

When the young wolf-dog saw us coming, she began leaping and tugging at the end of her chain. She had a propensity for making a bad
impression on people, and today was no exception.

"This is Kayak. She's half wolf," I said proudly. I reached to calm her,
but her chain broke and she came racing between us, the length of chain
flying out behind her. Dixie and Deanna scattered away, yelling in
fright, as my wolf raced around the corner of the house.

Embarrassed, I rushed after her and nearly bumped into Patrick,
coming the other way. He made a grab at Kayak as she sped past and
managed to step on the end of the chain. That stopped her with a
sudden jerk, but she swung happily back and slapped her black tail
on our legs.

"You're a bad dog!" I scolded.

"Here," my brother said. "You hold her while I fix it."

We pulled a reluctant Kayak back to her doghouse. Patrick produced
a piece of wire from his pocket, so I held the dog's collar while my
brother fastened the broken chain back together.

Dixie and Deanna approached cautiously. Kayak stood quietly, almost
ominously, her tail low and still as she eyed the two girls with suspicion.

"She won't hurt you," I promised. "She's only a puppy and she's gentle."

"Okay," Dixie said, taking a couple of steps nearer. "I just love dogs."

Kayak growled. Dixie stopped.

"There, that should hold!" Patrick stood up decisively, and I let go of
Kayak. She tugged at her chain, but it held. Frustrated, she howled after
us as we walked back around to the front porch. Patrick went into the
house, and the girls and I dropped onto the steps and sat in silence for a
few minutes.

"Why do you homeschool?" Dixie asked finally, grasping desperately
for some topic of conversation.

"I bet it's easier." Deanna kicked the ground.

I had a sudden vision of my parents sitting in the living room and
opening my history book with the cheery direction, "Okay. Tell us the

names of the first five presidents, along with all the major events that happened during each presidency."

"No," I said honestly, "I don't think it's really easier. But that isn't why we homeschool. We're Christians. My parents believe that God wants them to give us a Christian education, and they'd rather teach us at home than send us to Christian school."

"I don't think there is a God." With that surprising announcement, Deanna leaned back against the wall and surveyed me coolly.

"Deanna!" Dixie gasped. "Don't say that!" She threw me an apologetic look.

"Why not?" Deanna said. "Maybe it's true. What makes you think there is one?"

Shocked, I groped for an answer. Why did I believe in God? I'd never thought about it. I'd just believed. "Lord, help me," I prayed silently.

Through my confusion, I heard Dixie hiss at her sister. "Deanna, stop it. People have got a right to believe whatever they want."

I knew both of them were wrong. I knew that there had to be a God. I knew there had to be truth, and that it didn't just depend on what somebody *wanted* to believe. I just couldn't explain why. Suddenly, the words from a Bible verse that I'd memorized years ago popped into my head.

"I believe by faith," I said triumphantly. "The Bible says in Hebrews 11:1 that 'faith is the assurance of things hoped for, the conviction of things not seen.' So, even if I can't see God, I know He's there."

Both girls gazed at me—Dixie with a puzzled frown, Deanna with a dubious expression. I trembled slightly, almost as if I had a fever. As soon as the words left my mouth, I suddenly felt hollow inside. Was faith really enough for me to run my life by? What if I was making some awful mistake? What if there wasn't a God at all?

Deanna brushed her hair back from her face. "Well, I guess I want something I can *see*."

Dixie just looked embarrassed.

To my relief, the front door of the cabin suddenly opened and all the adults came out toward the Morrises' car. We joined them, and Mrs. Morris smiled at me.

"How nice you're the same ages!" she said. "You'll have to come down for a visit soon."

"That would be fun!" Dixie beamed, a little too widely. Her sister just climbed into the car without a word.

That would be awful, I thought, trying to smile.

Then they were gone, leaving me standing alone on the dusty driveway. The hot sun beat down on my head and I felt almost dizzy. Not only did Deanna—one of our very few neighbors—seem to hate me for some unknown reason, but I felt as if a big part of my world lay in shambles around my feet. I'd always believed in God, but what if there wasn't a God after all? How could I know?

Chapter 7: The Noise in the Woods

Why do I believe in God? The question flashed across my mind as soon as I opened my eyes the next morning. I groaned, cuddling Parka close to my chin as the cat purred softly. "What a question!" I told my sleepy Siamese. "Why did Deanna have to ask that?"

I had been a Christian since I was four or five years old, and no one had ever challenged me with a question like that before. Believing in God seemed as natural as eating or breathing. I could remember praying and hearing Bible stories almost all my life. What if God didn't exist? It seemed that my entire world had fallen apart—like the house built on nothing but sand in one of Jesus' parables.

I wanted to talk to my mother about it, but the whole morning was a whirl of unpacking more stuff and washing the kitchen floor. While I did that, Mom made a trip into Torch Heights for groceries and fresh drinking water. We didn't have a well at Steller's Creek and it wasn't safe to drink the creek water. Sometimes when people drink water straight from a stream without boiling it or chlorinating it, they can get horribly sick. We wanted to avoid that! In the winter we planned to boil much of our drinking water, but the summer weather was so hot that we hated to build a fire in the wood stove very much. The next summer, we planned to drill a well.

Anyway, I hoped to talk to Mom when she returned, but she had news for me that drove all the questions out of my head for the moment.

"Jessica, you have a letter!" In spite of her armful of groceries, Mom managed to wave the pink envelope at me as she came in the door.

"A letter?" I recognized the curly, painstaking handwriting at once—my best friend from the homeschool group in Kalispell. "It's from Maria!"

Eagerly I hurried out to the porch, tore the envelope open, and plopped down on the front step.

> Dear Jessica,
>
> How are you? Do you like your new house? Have you made any new friends? It's lonely here without you.
>
> Camp was fun, but I missed you awfully. We did some crafts, but nothing new. Remember when you accidentally superglued your sweatshirt to the back of your shorts?
>
> The speaker was good. He had a lot of pictures of other countries, since he is also a missionary. They had an altar call, and asked everyone who wanted to be a missionary to come up in front. You'll never believe this, but I went forward, too. I'm going to be a missionary nurse.

My mouth dropped open in surprise. Maria was right. I did have a hard time picturing my orderly and predictable friend volunteering for missions, let alone actually doing it. Why, Maria didn't even like to sleep in a tent! I turned the page. She went on for another paragraph about the missionary, then switched back to my move.

> Are there lots of bugs there at your new house? Should I bring bug spray when I come to visit you in September?
>
> I am really excited about seeing you again. Mom says that maybe I can bring my schoolbooks when I come, so that I can stay longer.

Guess what? I'm going to study German this year. It should be fun. That way I can start writing to my cousins and Grandmother in Germany.

Please write soon. I miss you awfully.

Love, Maria.

I carefully folded up the letter again and tucked it into my pocket.

"Well, how's Maria?" Mom was still putting away the groceries, and she looked up with a smile as I came into the kitchen. Patrick munched on potato chips at the table.

I told them Maria's astounding news.

"She'd probably make a good nurse," Mom commented. "She's so neat and organized."

"She's antiseptic," Patrick interjected.

"Patrick!" I said, "She is not!"

My brother raised both hands in surrender. "All I meant is that she likes to keep things clean! That's a good thing for a nurse!"

He did have a point there. Maria would never have spilled superglue on *her* sweatshirt and then sat on it.

I let that pass and got to the burning question. "Mom, do you think Maria could visit for a whole week, or maybe two? Her mom said she could bring her schoolbooks with her."

"I think so," Mom sounded cheerful. "Double-check with Dad but it's okay with me."

To my great delight, Dad agreed, too. After I finished my chores around the kitchen and hauled in a bucket of creek water to wash dishes in, I climbed up to my loft and spent the rest of the afternoon writing to Maria with the good news.

After dinner, Penny came to spend the evening since her dad was working a late shift at the mill, and her mother had to coordinate a game night at the nursing home. Penny had decided that she'd rather visit me than play Bingo! As always, my friend was full of plans.

"Have you ever gone fishing in the creek?" she called, halfway up the ladder to my loft.

"No," I said hopefully, looking down at her.

"Do you want to?"

"Sure! But I don't have a pole, unless Patrick will lend us his."

"Let's ask him." Penny dropped back to the floor. "Otherwise we can share mine."

I got permission from my mother (along with a warning not to go too far so late in the day) and we skipped happily from the house. Penny grabbed her pole from where she'd tossed it on the porch. St. Peter, who never strayed far from Penny, swooped low over our heads and dragged his crow-feet through my hair. I shrieked and ducked as the bird flew ahead of us, turning a barrel roll in the air. He was always fun to watch because he seemed to enjoy flying so much.

"Okay," Penny said. "Where's brother Pat?"

"Probably in his shop. Let's go ask him!"

We skipped together to the wooden shed behind the house, and I pushed the creaky door open. Patrick stood inside, bent over something on his big wooden table. He held a wood-burning tool in his hand, but before I could see what he was doing, he jumped back from the table and nearly pushed me out the door.

"Hey!" I protested in surprise. "Let me in!"

"Hey, yourself!" Patrick planted himself firmly in front of the door. "You're supposed to knock first!"

Puzzled, I looked at him, wondering why that upset him so much. I rarely knocked when entering the shop, of all places! As I opened my mouth to make an angry retort, I suddenly remembered that Penny was standing there. I also remembered Mom's frequent admonition that "a gentle answer turns away wrath." Whether it was Penny's presence or Mom's influence, I don't know, but I managed to say meekly, "I'm sorry."

Patrick glanced at Penny who was cheerfully watching the whole encounter. "I'm sorry for getting so upset," he apologized. "Just knock next time, okay? Did you see anything?"

More confused than ever, I echoed, "See anything?"

"Oh, never mind." He went back inside and locked the door.

"Patrick!" I yelled, banging on it. "Can I borrow your fishing pole?"

Well, even after all that, my brother would not lend us his pole. He'd gotten it for his birthday, along with a nice bunch of tackle, and he absolutely refused to let me take it along. So, we ended up with just Penny's pole. We dug some worms under logs at the edge of the forest, carefully tucked them in an old can full of dirt, and tied Kayak up so she wouldn't scare the fish. After almost an hour, Penny and I finally set off down a path that ran along Steller's Creek.

It wasn't much of a trail I discovered, as we scrambled over several big fallen logs and pushed our way under boughs. In the end, the path disappeared entirely when we reached a thicket of tangled red willows, alders, and raspberry bushes near the stream.

"We go this way!" Penny confidently struck off into the trees to work her way around the thicket, and I followed. We squeezed through clumps of twisting alders and found ourselves on the creek bank, just upstream from a fallen log that stretched across the water. The creek was wider there, and a calm pool had formed above the log.

We carefully baited the hook and put the line in the water, propping the pole against some rocks. Then we plopped back on the bank to wait, watching the evening sunlight glance off the water. The line floated downstream a bit, then held steady, moving only slightly with the gentle eddy of the creek.

"Have you ever been to camp?" Penny asked suddenly, after we'd been sitting quietly for several minutes.

"Church camp?"

"Yeah."

"Yes," I said, dropping a dead leaf into the water and watching it swirl downstream. "Almost every summer except this one, because we moved." With a pang of loneliness, I thought again about Maria, and how we'd roomed together every year until this summer.

"I'm going next week," Penny said. "I thought I couldn't go this year, but Mom and Dad have enough money after all. I just found out today!"

"You're leaving?" I looked at her in dismay.

She nodded, excitement shining in her eyes. "It's so neat! We have little cabins on a lake, and go swimming every day. One night they have fireworks over the water."

At my church camp, we had no lake. We roomed in big dormitories and played miniature golf in our free time. Although Maria and I thoroughly enjoyed our experiences, Penny's camp sounded wonderful, too. As she chattered on about all the fun she expected, I swallowed hard, trying to get rid of the lump in my throat. I couldn't imagine a whole week without Penny.

"And then we sit around the fire and tell ghost stories," she added, her eyes widening and her voice dropping. "And then we have to walk back through the dark to our cabins with just flashlights."

A little spooked, I looked around. My parents didn't allow us to tell ghost stories, and I disliked the thought of hearing them around a campfire late at night.

"One year we saw a Sasquatch," Penny continued. "You know, Bigfoot?"

"You saw Bigfoot?" I said, jiggling the fishing pole a little and trying to see the worm bob under the surface of the water.

"Well, we think it was one," she said. "Me and Karen went out after dark, and we heard something crashing through the trees after us. We ran as fast as we could back to the cabin, and then looked out the window, and we saw something black disappear into the trees. Our counselor thought somebody was trying to scare us, but I think it was a Sasquatch."

Her lowered voice and confident tone alarmed me. I shivered. She shivered too but kept right on going.

"Did you know there was a Sasquatch in Glacier Park? It came up and shook some camper's trailer back and forth and back and forth for a long time one night. He was too scared to open the door. Finally, it disappeared when the sun came up."

Glacier Park was less than fifty miles from Steller's Creek.

I looked around uneasily. "Penny," I said, "It's starting to get dark."

She looked around at the darkening water and deepening shadows. Then we stared at each other with wide eyes. "Let's go!" she quavered.

We reeled in the fishing line, grabbed our can of bait, and started back through the trees. In a few moments, we found ourselves on the trail and paused to catch our breath. Then we heard it.

Deep in the willow thicket, as if something heavy had stepped on it, a branch cracked. Penny and I stood paralyzed for a second.

"Don't move!" I whispered, just as Penny screamed and started running up the trail toward the house.

Chapter 8: More Scared of You

I fled after Penny. I don't remember how I scrambled over the logs that blocked the trail. I know that Penny fell once. I yanked her to her feet, and we just kept tearing along as fast as we could go. Seconds later we staggered into the clearing by my house, our hair full of dead twigs and our legs scratched by wild rose bushes. Amazingly, Penny still clutched her pole in one hand, but I'd dropped the worm can somewhere along the path.

From the corner of my eye, I saw Lady race out of the trees behind us, running for all she was worth. She passed Penny and me, beat us to the house, and ran straight around it to vanish under the porch. Only a second behind the dog, we dashed across the porch into the kitchen, pulled the door shut behind us, and leaned, panting, against it.

Startled, Kayak scrambled to her feet. Dad looked up from tuning his violin, and Mom nearly dropped her book. "What's the matter?" she exclaimed.

Penny and I looked at each other.

Finally, I spoke. "We heard a noise—"

"It was a Sasquatch!" Penny interjected, at the same time.

"A what?" Patrick poked his head out of his loft and looked down.

"What kind of noise?" Dad asked calmly, rubbing his small brick of rosin slowly up the violin bow. He turned the bow carefully in his hand, testing it.

"A stick cracked," I said. "It broke in the thicket as we were walking back, and I felt like something was watching us."

My parents looked doubtfully at us.

"We didn't see anything," Penny admitted.

"Just a stick? You didn't hear anything else?" Dad asked.

"A Sasquatch?" Patrick was laughing so hard that he nearly fell out of the loft.

"There *are* such things!" Penny defended herself.

"Lady followed you," Patrick said. "She snuck into the woods after you left. It was probably her."

"Well, then, what was *she* running from?" I demanded. "She was just as scared as we were."

Patrick laughed. Dad looked skeptical. Mom took us halfway seriously.

"Do you think it could have been a bear?" she asked.

"That's not very likely." Dad shook his head. "The Ruffins haven't seen a bear around here since they moved here ten years ago. It probably was a squirrel or Lady, since the dogs didn't bark or anything. Even if it had been a bear, it would be miles away by now. You girls probably scared it half to death."

"That's true," Mom added. "I'm sure it was more scared of you than you were of it!"

Dad lifted his violin to his shoulder and grinned at me as the instrument sang out the first few notes of "Kitchen Girl," one of my favorite fiddle tunes.

With a rueful smile, I led Penny up the ladder to my loft and shoved aside my deserted stationery as we plopped onto my bed.

"I don't think it was a squirrel," Penny confided with conviction.

"Me either."

I sighed, and we both fell silent. There didn't seem to be any more to say about that. After all, how could we prove that that old stick hadn't been cracked by a squirrel? And if it had been a bear, we probably terrified it. I had a sudden mental picture of a little bear running for home as fast as his fat legs could carry him, and I started to giggle.

"What's so funny?" Penny rolled over in surprise and sat up.

I tried to describe what I was laughing at, and Penny caught on. "And when he got home," she said in a growly voice. "Father Bear said 'those girls were probably more scared of you, than you were scared of them.'"

We both howled with laughter, and Lady barked impatiently at the bottom of the ladder. In the living room, Dad's fiddle broke into a rendition of "Fire on the Mountain." He always called that "Mariel's Song," because my mother had spent a summer in the mountains manning a fire tower and watching for forest fires. That's where my father met her, actually. He always said he never expected to find a Virginia "southern belle" in the Montana Rockies.

As I swung my legs back and forth, I accidentally kicked a dirty sock from underneath the bed—some of the laundry I had tried to hide from Deanna and Dixie a few days before. That reminded me of their visit, and I told Penny about it.

"Dixie's pretty nice," Penny agreed when I finished my account. "But Deanna is really mean. I fell off my bike in front of their house one time and cut both my knees. Deanna yelled at me for trespassing on their property, but then Dixie came outside and gave me a ride home."

I frowned, thinking of Deanna's question about God. Should I tell Penny that part of the story? I knew she was a Christian because we'd talked about it before and her family went to our new church, but I didn't want her to be upset like I was. Still, it would be nice to talk about it.

Unaware of my turmoil, Penny lay back on the floor, pointed her right foot at the ceiling, and slowly drew an imaginary circle. "I don't think they're Christians," she said all of sudden, surprising me because I didn't know she was thinking about the same thing. "Because Dixie has a rabbit's foot in her car, hanging from the mirror."

"Huh?"

"You know," Penny said. "A rabbit foot is supposed to be a good-luck charm. A Christian shouldn't have a good-luck charm because there's no such thing as luck. God takes care of us, not luck."

I understood what she meant, but somehow I felt that the rabbit foot wasn't a good indication of Dixie's lack of faith. After all, Dixie had sort of stuck up for me. I really didn't know what she thought. "I don't think she's a Christian either," I said slowly, trying to figure out how to explain. "But sometimes people have those things, like rabbit's feet, because they just think they're pretty, not because they want good luck."

"Yeah," Penny admitted. "I know."

We were both quiet a moment, and then she added, "I guess we should tell her that sometime."

"Tell her what?"

"About God and luck." Penny sat up with her typical enthusiasm.

"I guess," I agreed reluctantly.

"Yes," Penny nodded to herself with conviction. "That's what we should do."

I felt a sinking feeling in the pit of my stomach. I was half-afraid that Penny would suggest going to the Morris house right that minute. Although she might want to share her faith with Dixie, I felt so confused that I wouldn't know what to say. What if Deanna asked more questions? I couldn't face that challenging stare again. Besides, I definitely didn't want Dixie hanging around, giggling and trying to get Patrick's attention. At that point, all I really wanted to do was stay as far away from the Morrises as I could!

Chapter 9: Oh, No, Not Again!

Penny left for camp on Sunday afternoon, leaving me alone with my family at Steller's Creek. Sunday was okay because we stayed busy. I managed to push Deanna's question to the back of my mind and concentrated on entertaining some visitors from our new church—a young couple with three toddlers.

Monday, though, started off all wrong. First Mom and Dad left for town to haul water again, leaving Patrick and me alone. My brother was mad because Dad told both of us to clean up the trash beside the cabin. The garbage can had been knocked over and Kayak and Lady appeared to be the culprits.

"I don't see how it could have been Lady," Patrick grumbled at me while we collected the cans and paper strewn around the yard. "She's with me all the time except when I tie her."

"Well, I don't see how it could have been Kayak!" I snapped back. "She was tied, too, except when she slept in the house last night."

"They both slept in the house last night."

"I suppose now you'll blame Parka! Well, she didn't do it either! She slept on my bed!"

We worked in silence for a few minutes.

"We need another trash bag," Patrick said.

I knew that he meant that I should get it, but I had no intention of doing so. "They're in the cardboard box beside the kitchen stove," I retorted. "Get one yourself!"

Patrick stomped off, as I struggled to jam the lid down on the can. It hardly fit. I figured that Kayak could easily knock it off—if she really was guilty. Frowning, I looked around and spied the woodpile at the corner of the house. Perfect!

I lugged a short, heavy chunk of wood over and plunked it on the top of the can. As I straightened up, I thought I caught a glimpse of something big and dark moving in the woods. I blinked. It was gone. Had it just been my imagination? I squinted, thinking about Penny's Sasquatch. Nothing moved. The sunlight shone through the trees, and the air hung heavily with summer heat, but I shivered with a chill of apprehension.

"Caw...Ha! Ha! Ha!" With a shriek of laughter, Penny's crow suddenly swooped down and landed on the trash can beside me, almost scaring me "spitless" (as one of my uncles in Idaho used to say).

"St. Peter!" I exclaimed, "What are you doing here? Do you miss Penny, too?"

St. Peter cocked his head, gazing at me with a bright black eye. Then he rubbed his beak on his feathers, chuckling quietly to himself.

"Did you make a mess of the trash?" I asked. "Well, you won't do it again—not with this can all loaded down with wood."

"They weren't by the stove—" Patrick broke off in mid-sentence, as he came back around the corner with another black trash bag in his hand. He stopped abruptly, hands on his hips, and looked at the log I had moved.

"How are we supposed to get the garbage in the can now?" he demanded, eyeing my handiwork. "Move the woodpile every time?"

I glared at him. "You figure it out!"

I aimed a kick at an empty coffee can, sending St. Peter flapping into the air in alarm. Then I marched back around the house and slammed the front door so loudly that the dishes on the counter rattled. With some satisfaction, I slipped home the big bolt to lock the door. Then I made myself a peanut butter sandwich.

Fifteen minutes later, Patrick pounded on the door. "Jessica! Let me in!"

I ignored him, although I did feel a little guilty.

"I'm going to tell Dad!" he said, glaring at me through the kitchen window. I stuck out my tongue. Patrick disappeared.

With sudden unease, I remembered the back door. I thought it was locked. Just in case, though, I ran down the narrow, dark hallway to check. Our back door didn't have a regular lock with a key, or even a big bolt like our front door. Instead, it had a sort of latch—a slim piece of metal with a knob on one end. The latch was fastened to the doorframe at one end, and I dropped the knobbed part into a hook on the door to lock it. Satisfied, I marched back to the kitchen.

After a few minutes of awful quiet, I began to wonder where Patrick had gone and to think about what my parents would say when they got home. A disturbing thought! As a matter of fact, I had just decided to open the front door when a small scratching sound came from the back of the house.

With sudden trepidation, I tiptoed down the hallway in time to see a tiny screwdriver poke through the narrow crack between the door and the frame. Horrified, I watched it wiggle around and then slide up toward the metal latch. With a couple of jerks, the screwdriver dislodged the latch, unlocking the door.

I dashed to the front of the house and desperately tried to unbolt the front door, but Patrick caught me. He swung half a bucket of water in one hand as he grabbed my arm with the other, cornering me against the still-locked door. Lady, who had followed him down the hall, barked hysterically at both of us, not sure whether to bite me or Patrick .

"Don't throw water in the house!" I screamed, grasping at one of Mom's rules for the faintest chance of escape.

Whether he would have dumped the bucket or not, I don't know. Just at that moment, somebody knocked on the door that I was leaning against. Patrick and I both froze. Neither of us had heard a vehicle. Had our parents returned already?

"You're in trouble now," I whispered.

"So are you," Patrick muttered back. "You didn't finish your chores either."

"I'm sorry for being cross!" I whispered desperately, low enough that I couldn't be heard on the porch. Hopefully Mom and Dad wouldn't know we'd been fighting. At least we could tell them we had "solved the problem."

"Me, too," Patrick said.

We looked unhappily at each other. Why did we always fight when our parents were gone?

Someone knocked again. "Hello? Is anyone home?"

It didn't sound like my mother. It sounded like—oh, no, it couldn't be.

Patrick took a step back, still holding the bucket, and I opened the door. On the porch stood Dixie Morris. In her slim new blue jeans and pink blouse, she looked as if she had just pranced off the cover of a magazine. I became suddenly conscious of my one red sock and one green sock, blue shorts, and yellow shirt. (One of the things Mom was doing in town was laundry because we didn't have a washing machine.)

"Hi!" our neighbor said brightly, looking at Patrick.

"Hi," my brother muttered, running his left hand self-consciously through his dark hair. "Sorry we didn't hear you coming."

"That's okay," Dixie said with a friendly smile.

After a pause, I mustered enough courtesy to invite Dixie into the house. Looking uncharacteristically embarrassed, Patrick sort of nodded as he sidled around her and went outside, carrying the bucket and dragging a growling Lady who apparently hadn't heard Dixie arrive either.

I closed the door after the pair, just as Kayak meandered purposefully down the hall from the back door. She slipped gracefully through the kitchen, eyed the food on the counter, and detoured past the wastebasket, missing nothing. Then, to my surprise, she swaggered over to Dixie, wagging her tail and sniffing. Watching her, I almost sniffed involuntarily, too, but caught myself. Dixie's perfume hung heavily in the air.

"Kayak, outside!" I ordered, opening the door again.

Rather reluctantly, Kayak went out. Dixie and I looked awkwardly at each other for a moment.

"Would you like some lemonade?" I offered.

"Sure!" She beamed at me, obviously relieved. She settled herself in a kitchen chair while I searched the cupboards for a glass. Fortunately, we hadn't taken the jar of lemonade back to the creek yet. Although warm, it would have to do.

"Deanna and Mom went to Kalispell," Dixie volunteered. "So I thought I'd drop in and say hi."

She looked so calm and collected, sitting there, oblivious to the turmoil that she and her sister stirred up inside me. I held my tongue and managed a smile as I poured the lemonade.

"That was nice of you."

Dixie looked down at the blue tablecloth, then back at me. "I wanted to apologize for Deanna." Her voice was low, and she suddenly looked uncertain. "She shouldn't have said what she said when we were here, and I'm sorry." Her eyes were hopeful as she studied my face.

Shocked, I stood still for a moment. Apologize? For Deanna? I pulled myself together, conscious of the anxious blue eyes.

"It's okay," I said.

"We do believe in God," Dixie said. "I mean we go to church at Christmas and stuff."

She seemed to be trying to get me to give her an answer to some question that I didn't understand. Puzzled, I just nodded.

"That's okay," I finally said again.

"Good." Dixie relaxed visibly, leaning back in her chair with a sigh. She changed the subject, chatting for awhile about her old home and the stables where she rode horses. That surprised me because Dixie didn't look like an outdoors person at all. She also told me about swimming competitions and her other school activities.

I politely chatted back and asked questions, surprised at how well the conversation was going. Actually, it wasn't bad at all without Deanna there. I wondered again why Dixie was being so friendly. She probably really wanted to see Patrick, I decided.

"When I go back this fall—" she started once, but suddenly cut herself off in mid-sentence.

Going back? Moving? Maybe I'd only have to put up with the Morrises for a couple of months! But Deanna had mentioned junior high in Torch Heights, hadn't she?

"Oh, are you going back?" I managed to ask casually. This sounded almost too good to be true. I really didn't want to run into Deanna ever, ever again.

Dixie hesitated. "I don't know."

I just looked at her, puzzled, and an awkward silence crept over both of us.

"Well, I want to go back," she said finally. "But we don't have our house there anymore. We had to sell it."

A faint look of hurt crept over her face, but she didn't give any further explanations. Instead she jumped up briskly. "I need to go! I've got stuff to do before Mom and Deanna get home. Maybe we can go hiking or something sometime. Have you ever been up to the lookout?"

"No."

The Lost Soul fire lookout could be seen from Penny's treehouse, but I'd never actually been to it. Penny and I hoped to take a long bike ride up there some afternoon, perhaps with a picnic lunch.

"Maybe we can drive up sometime," Dixie offered. "It's not far."

"I'll have to ask my parents," I said pleasantly.

"Great!" Dixie took that for a positive answer. "I'll see you later!"

I waved as she zipped out of the driveway in her green car (as fast as she could zip on the dusty, rutted road). Then I wandered back into the house. While I felt a tiny bit flattered that a high school junior would want to be my friend, I suspected that she might be just trying to get Patrick's attention. The girls at our Kalispell church did that sometimes, and I hated it. I wanted friends who liked me for me, not for my brother! Besides, unfortunately, I couldn't have Dixie for a friend without running into her younger sister.

While part of me was glad Dixie had apologized, the apology couldn't answer Deanna's nagging question. Why did I believe in God? How could I know for sure?

Chapter 10: To Give an Account

 "Bother that Deanna!" I muttered, closing the cabin door behind me. "I hope they do go back to Missoula!"

After cleaning the kerosene lamps and finishing up my other assigned chores, I decided that the day was too beautiful for me to stay in the cabin. So, I climbed into my loft just long enough to grab my Bible. As I came out the front door again, Kayak met me on the porch, her ears erect and tail poised.

"Do you want to go for a walk?" I asked.

An energetic leap off the porch answered that question! First I went to tell Patrick where I was going since my parents had given me strict orders not to wander too far away alone. I found my brother in front of his shop, trying to take apart a bicycle tire.

"Hi!" I said brightly, hoping he wasn't mad anymore. "What's that for?"

Patrick hadn't heard me coming. He turned in surprise, blocking my view of the interior of the shop as he kicked the door closed behind him.

"Oh, an experiment," he evaded. "Did your friend leave?"

"*My* friend!" I said. "More like *your* friend, maybe."

"What do you mean?"

"Oh, never mind." I might as well not get into that.

Patrick gave me a funny look, but didn't pursue the topic.

"I'm going for a walk," I said. "Is your shop all fixed up?"

"Yeah." Patrick still blocked my way.

"Can I see how you arranged it?" I tried to peek around him.

"Ah, not yet." My brother bent his head over the tire again.

Not wanting to renew the fight of the morning, I didn't push it. Why was he acting so mysterious, though? This was the second time he wouldn't let me in.

"You're not building another rocket?" I asked. A few years ago, he'd almost blown up our garage. My grandpa said that Patrick would someday destroy us all with his experiments, but my brother hadn't built anything too reckless since that rocket.

"No, of course not!"

I looked at him in silence for a moment. Then a light began to dawn, and I struggled to suppress a smile. My birthday! Patrick must be building something for my birthday next week. What could it be? New bookshelves? Perhaps a window seat for my loft? What could the tire be for? In any case, it must be a surprise. I decided not to let on that I knew— well, sort of knew, anyway.

"I'm going for a walk up there." I pointed to the top of the hill toward the treehouse.

"Okay," Patrick said, as if he hoped I'd go away.

Trying to hide my suspicions, I just beamed at my big brother, whistled to Kayak, and set off toward the hilltop. St. Peter swooped after us, sailing into the forest with a triumphant crow-cackle. Just as we entered the trees, I looked back. Patrick had disappeared inside the shop, and Lady lay in front of the building, nose on paws, waiting for him to re-emerge.

With a sigh, I looked wistfully at my energetic wolf-dog. "I wish you liked me as much as Lady likes Patrick," I told her. Kayak tipped her head to one side and studied my face. "You didn't come because you wanted to be with me. You just wanted to go for a walk. You'd be just as happy all by yourself."

Kayak's white-masked face looked saucy as she tossed her head, gave a little jump, and bounced ahead of me up the trail. I followed, enjoying her fun as she ranged from side to side, investigating stumps, logs, and tufts of grass with her curious black nose. Some dogs snuffled, but Kayak seemed silent and calculating. I suspected that she was hunting for mice. She'd caught them before.

I smiled to myself. In spite of her unruly streak of independence, Kayak was so smart—a wonderful leader for my future sled dog team. I closed my eyes for a moment, envisioning Kayak fearlessly leading my team of huskies over the ice-blue Alaskan snow, responding swiftly to my shouted commands as we negotiated the treacherous terrain. Maybe I'd be a dogsled missionary, carrying medicine to remote villages.

Then reality stepped in. Not only did I live in Montana, miles from Alaska, but I owned only one dog—who still needed basic training. At this point, she barely grasped the command to sit!

"And I need to get a dogsled," I said aloud. "So you can learn to really pull." My wolf-dog looked at me merrily and bounced away.

We climbed until I found the perfect spot for my Bible study—the giant old log overgrown with green moss that I had discovered on my first morning at Steller's Creek. I seated myself on it and looked back toward our house, but I couldn't see it because of the trees. St. Peter had disappeared. Kayak rustled around in the bushes at the edge of the clearing, and I felt comfortably alone.

The air was clear and clean. The trees fell away below me, opening up a view of the distant valley. Off to my right, miles away, I spotted the tiny black shape of the Lost Soul fire tower, perched precariously on the edge of a rocky, reddish precipice. Even farther away, beyond Lost Soul Mountain, I could barely make out the misty, blue Canadian Rockies, capped with snow. They were so faint, they seemed almost dream-like. I felt a sudden, indefinable longing to go there, to climb to the top, to somehow understand something.

"Ka-ronk! Ka-ronk!" Above me, a flock of Canada geese (a gaggle of geese, according to my mom, and she should know) winged their way toward Deep Lake, a few miles from our house. They flew steadily, purposefully, their long black necks gracefully arched as they called to one another with haunting honking.

After the geese faded to pencil outlines against the sky, I sighed and opened my Bible. My parents had ruled that Patrick and I each read four chapters a week somewhere in the Bible. Then they wanted us to explain what we learned. With the busy weeks of moving and unpacking, I had fallen behind.

Kayak bopped her nose against my leg, as if to reassure me of her presence, then wandered off again.

Carefully I paged to 1 Peter and started to read chapter three. I read the verses about wives and husbands a bit fast, but got tangled a bit when I found the next part about seeking peace and being harmonious. Somehow I suspected that I hadn't been very harmonious that morning. Then I reached verse fifteen:

> But sanctify Christ as Lord in your hearts, always being ready to make a defense to everyone who asks you to give an account for the hope that is in you, yet with gentleness...

I stared at the words for a moment. With a groan, I put my head down on my knees. "That fits me," I said aloud to nobody. "I need be able to defend what I believe, but I don't know the answer. When Deanna asked why I believe in God, I couldn't tell her. Oh, Lord, are you really out there?"

In all my life, nobody had ever challenged me like Deanna had. My parents became Christians when I was four years old, and I soon followed in their footsteps. I couldn't even remember a time before I'd known and loved God and tried sincerely to obey Him. Why, if He didn't exist—stubbornly, I refused to think any more along *that* line. He must exist! He had to! How could I know for sure?

Angrily, I kicked the log with my heel. Why did Deanna have to come along and upset my world?

Suddenly, through the turmoil of my thoughts, I became aware of a new noise. I lifted my head and half-turned in my seat to see Kayak across the little clearing. The wolf-dog was barking, first on one side of a cluster of pine trees, then racing around to bark on the other. I strained to see what she had found, but couldn't make out anything.

Then, among the tree trunks and bushes, something long and brown moved. Just as I jumped to my feet, a tall, gangly creature with a humped back thumped out of the thicket followed by a long-legged baby. Two Roman noses, almost ridiculous in length, turned briefly in my direction, but I don't think either moose actually saw me because Kayak was practically underfoot.

The animals stood still for a split second. The next instant they turned and ran into the trees and up the mountain at an unbelievable speed. Their rolling gait and long legs looked hilarious. At that moment, though, nothing seemed funny, because a wildly excited Kayak disappeared into the trees right after the moose, in hot and furious pursuit.

I jumped to my feet, dropping my Bible on the log.

"Kayak!" I screamed after her. "Kayak, come back here!"

My voice echoed from the red cliffs across the valley.

Chapter 11: Home from the Hill

Leaving my Bible where I had dropped it, I raced after my wolf-dog and the two moose. A few more frustrated barks came from the depths of the forest. I ran in the direction of the sound, pushing past the pine trees, tripping over logs, and catching my hair in branches.

Finally stumbling into another tiny clearing, I found myself painfully knee-deep in wild rose bushes. On a nearby tree, a small red squirrel stared balefully at me from a branch. Then it scurried around the trunk, peeked at me again, and began chattering. Far off in the distance, I heard another hysterical bark.

"Kayak!" I screamed again, both furious and worried. "Kayak! Come here! Bad dog!"

From the cliffs my voice echoed back. "Yak, ome ear, oh…"

"Jessica? Jessica!"

Something came crashing through the trees after me. I turned just as Lady bounded into the clearing, my brother stumbling behind her. Spying me, Lady leaped through the bushes and pressed up against my legs, her tail wagging furiously.

"What's the matter?" Patrick hollered, slowing down when he saw me. "What are you screaming about?"

"Kayak ran after a moose and her calf!"

"Oh, no!" Patrick's face reflected both relief and concern as he gasped for breath. "I thought you were hurt. Which way did she go?"

I pointed and we started off together, too tired to run anymore, but stopping often to whistle and call. Since Kayak was still rather small, she probably wouldn't hurt the moose calf, I reasoned. I was more afraid that the enraged mother would flail out at my dog with her heavy hooves. I could just picture my crazy pup prancing around the pair—the frightened baby and the furious mother with eyes blazing fire.

"Oh, Lord," I prayed desperately in silence. "Please bring Kayak back!"

Patrick and I walked for almost an hour, calling again and again. Occasionally we heard Kayak bark in the distance, but the sound grew fainter and fainter. Eventually, we couldn't hear her at all.

"Well," my older brother said finally, "I think we'd better go back to the house."

"But what if she gets hurt or lost?" I wailed.

"We can't find her now," he pointed out. "She could be anywhere, and I don't think she'll come back until she's tired of chasing the moose."

Reluctantly, I turned to follow him. Suddenly the sky, so cheerfully blue earlier, seemed hard and cold. The wind picked up and I shivered.

My brother looked at me sympathetically. "Don't worry," he offered. "She'll find her way back. She's pretty smart, you know."

I didn't answer. Things seemed hopeless. I imagined my carefree pup lying injured among the pine trees, unable to limp her way home. What if she got lost and just wandered through the woods, hungry and lonesome, until she starved to death?

My thoughts drifted back to when Kayak was a little bundle of fur. I'd brought her home when she was six weeks old, and she cried and howled at night. She slept in a carton in the kitchen, and I spent hours sitting beside her box, trying to soothe her until she went to sleep. As soon as it seemed safe, I'd tiptoe back to my room to sleep until she woke up and howled again. If I lost her, I told myself, I'd never want another dog.

Mom and Dad still weren't home when we got back to the cabin, so Patrick went out to his woodshop and I crashed on the couch and flipped on the little, battery-powered radio, hoping for some music to cheer me up. Instead, I caught the ending of some religious broadcast.

"Thou shalt not test the Lord your God!" the radio boomed. I sat up with a jerk, my attention caught by the minister's authoritative voice.

"The Israelites tested God and they were destroyed by fire, by plague," the strong voice continued emphatically. "Christ, when tempted by the Father of Lies, replied, 'Thou shalt not test the Lord Thy God.' Today, as we go forth, let us be faithful, that we too may not test the Lord our God. Our Heavenly Father—"

The minister launched into a prayer and I sat in stunned silence for moment before switching the radio off again.

"Oh, Father!" I wailed. "Am I testing You by wondering if You're really even there?"

It seemed as if my questions just kept piling up and boiling around in my head. Worn out by all the stresses of the long day, I buried my face in the couch pillow and cried until I heard our truck pull into the driveway.

By the time I got outside, Patrick had told our parents what happened to Kayak. They seemed worried, too.

"Were you watching her?" Dad asked.

"Yes, I was," I insisted. "I was reading, and I kept looking up to check on her every couple minutes. When she found the moose, she wasn't that far away, but she wouldn't come back when I called."

"Well," Mom sighed. "I'm glad that *you* didn't discover the moose. Kayak may have kept you from getting hurt."

"Do you think she'll get hurt?" I asked, hoping that somehow they could know.

"I hope not," Dad said. "Probably she'll get tired out and come home."

My mother put her arm around me, comfortingly. "Why don't we pray?"

So we all bowed our heads while Dad asked the Lord to protect my little wolf-dog and bring her safely home. Then we decided to look for Kayak again right after supper.

As it turned out, we didn't need to look. Just as Patrick was putting the last little bit of all the toppings onto the last taco shell (his grand finale to dinner), we heard an unusual movement on the front porch and Lady started barking. I jumped up and opened the door.

There, head hanging guiltily, stood the wolf-dog. When she saw me, she wagged her tail tentatively.

"It's Kayak!" I called out. Then I reeled back and put my hand over my nose. "And I think she got into a skunk!"

Well, needless to say, Kayak smelled awful, but that fact didn't seem to bother her nearly as much as it bothered us. We guessed that she had either rolled in a dead skunk, or been sprayed mildly by a live one.

After dinner I put on old clothes, grabbed a bar of biodegradable soap, and marched down to the creek to give her a bath—several of them, in fact. Kayak came willingly enough, but she wiggled and jumped about in the clear water as if she didn't like the plan. By the time I finished, we were both soaked and cold. Kayak still smelled, and now I did, too.

"You know what?" I told her, shivering on the creek bank. "You still stink. Why do you always get into so much trouble?"

Kayak shook herself, spraying Lady with little drops of water. The Australian shepherd had watched the proceedings from the dry bank, occasionally whining with anxiety. "Look at Lady," I pointed out. "She never runs away. She never chases moose. She's never gotten skunky. Lady's a good dog."

Lady wagged her tail at the unexpected praise, but Kayak didn't care. At that moment, I guess I didn't either. I just knew that Kayak was my dog. I loved her and I was glad she was okay.

I looked up at the darkening sky, noticing the red streaks over the mountains in the west as the sun set. "Thank you, God," I said, forgetting my questions for the moment. "Thank you for bringing Kayak home."

I tied the protesting wolf-dog securely at the edge of the trees and headed for the cabin. Someone had lit the lanterns, and a warm glow came from the front windows. As I pushed open the door, I heard the hissing sound of the gasoline lanterns and smelled the popcorn that Mom was making on the propane stove. The kerosene lamps flickered in the center of the kitchen table. As quiet peace stole over me, a line from an old poem suddenly flashed into my head—"home is the hunter, home from the hill—" and I smiled with contentment.

"Do we have to run the generator to work the CB?" Patrick wanted to know. He and my father were bending over a project on the kitchen table, so I plopped down into another chair to see what they were doing.

"What's a generator?" I asked.

"We ordered one in Torch Heights." Dad didn't lift his head. He had taken the old CB apart and was wiring something together. "No, Patrick. It'll run off the batteries."

"But what is it?" I persisted.

"It's kind of like an engine," Dad said, picking at something inside the CB with a tiny screwdriver. "We'll use it to charge up car batteries, and then we can use those batteries to run lights, a radio, or a CB."

"Electric lights?" I asked eagerly.

"No," Patrick said with a straight face. "Methane lights."

"Oh," I said. I'd never heard of methane lights.

"Patrick's just teasing you." Mom came to the rescue, as she set the big, stainless steel bowl of popcorn on the table and handed us each a paper plate. "Of course they'll be electric."

I made a face at my brother and dove into the snack.

"Can you quit jiggling the table?" Dad looked up. "Take that popcorn in the living room, why don't you?"

We did, and Patrick pulled out our old checkerboard and persuaded me to play. Actually, that wasn't all that difficult. I have a faint hope that practice will eventually make perfect, and I will someday be a wonderful checker player. That has not happened yet, however.

"Which color?" My brother held out a red and a black checker.

"I don't see that it matters," I said. "You always win anyway."

"You're getting better, though," Patrick encouraged. "You just don't look before you move. You always fall right into the trap, even though it's obvious."

"One of these days I'll beat you," I said, with more confidence than I felt.

"Look," Patrick said helpfully, after I made the first move. "You should always put your first checker here, on the side. Then you can't be jumped. It's an advantageous position."

"Can I move it back and do it, even though I already moved?"

"Of course not!" He wasn't willing to let me go that far.

Less than ten minutes later, my brother pushed back his chair with a grin. "This is great! Nothing like winning with six kings!"

"There's nothing like losing to six kings," I moped. "Let's play again."

Two hours and many wins later, Patrick finally called it quits. Dad shut down the hissing lanterns, and we all went off to bed. After my long and exhausting day, I dropped off to sleep in seconds.

In the middle of the night, something woke me. I lay frozen in the darkness, listening.

The sound came again—a low, menacing growl from Lady, downstairs in the kitchen. I could hear the scrabble of toenails, and then Lady let out a tremendous volley of barking. Outside, tied to her doghouse, Kayak cut loose with a wild howl.

Chapter 12: Questions About Life

"Lady, be quiet!" Patrick's grumpy voice came through the darkness from his loft opposite mine.

Lady quieted to a growl, but Kayak kept right on barking, a note of hysteria in her howls.

I could hear thumping downstairs and the murmur of my parents' voices. A flashlight flickered, and I heard the familiar creak of the front door opening. After a moment, Dad yelled at Kayak to hush. The door banged shut again.

"Did you see anything?" Mom called out.

"No," Dad replied. "I don't know what they were so upset about. Maybe a deer ran through."

I couldn't make out my mother's reply.

"Kayak's just not used to sleeping outside here at night," Dad said. The flashlight flickered out.

I just yawned and promptly fell asleep again.

The next morning dawned a little cooler than usual, and it put my father in a firewood-gathering mood. At breakfast he announced that he wanted my help for the morning.

I looked up from buttering my toast. "Is Patrick coming, too?" I asked.

"I need to do some stuff in the shop," Patrick said. He, Mom, and Dad exchanged significant looks. Apparently they all knew what he was building. It must be something for my thirteenth birthday. It had to be! Maybe a window-seat for my loft? A new bookshelf?

"What do you have to do?" I asked innocently.

"Oh, things," Patrick said.

"I think we can manage a couple loads of wood without him," Dad said. "Why don't we have our Bible study first and then get going?"

Mom and Patrick cleared the table while I collected the Bibles from all over the house before we gathered around the table again. Lately we'd been reading from the book of Romans, but today Patrick volunteered that he had something to talk about.

"Sure," Dad said. "What is it?"

It turned out to be 2 Timothy 3:14-17. Most of the verses talked about the use of Scripture for teaching Christians about what is right. However, the first part especially jumped out at me.

> You, however, continue in the things you have learned and become convinced of...from childhood you have known the sacred writings which are able to give you the wisdom that leads to salvation through faith which is in Christ Jesus...

As my brother read aloud, my heart gave a sudden lift. I had known about God from childhood just as Timothy had. The verse seemed to say that I could understand my faith better by reading the Bible, as I had been doing on the day Kayak ran away. Maybe it *would* give me wisdom and help me to understand the truth. I must be on the right track.

Patrick found the verse interesting for a different reason. "I always thought I'd want to be a missionary," he said. "But I've been thinking lately that I'd like to be one who translates the Bible. I've been reading about how some missionaries spend years doing translations and how much it affects the people. It gives them God's words in their own language. Even after the missionary is gone, God's book still changes lives."

Still changes lives. For some reason, I suddenly remembered my father telling us about a famous author who decided to become an atheist. Before he did, though, that author thought he should read the Bible from beginning to end so he could be sure he *didn't* believe it. By the time he finished Revelation, he had become a Christian. I wondered if I should start with Genesis?

"Jessica?" Dad's voice pulled me out of my thoughts. "Do you have anything to share today?"

With a jerk, I focused back on the Bible study. I'd missed the rest of Patrick's comments.

"Ah, no," I stammered.

"Well, then, let's pray." Dad bowed his head.

After we finished, Patrick sauntered out the door, headed for his shop. Dad and I donned heavy canvas gloves and denim jackets and set out after wood in our big, old green truck. As soon as Lady saw us climbing in, she leaped into the back of the pickup.

"Can Kayak come, too?" I paused with a foot in the cab.

"Sure," Dad said. "Better have her inside or she'll jump out the back."

Sensing that permission had been granted, Kayak wiggled past me onto the seat.

"That's one nice thing about Lady," I said, scrambling in after my wolf-dog. "She'll stay in the truck—most of the time, anyway!"

The gray Aussie was already running from side to side in the truck bed. As the vehicle began to move, she stood on her hind legs and put her nose in the crack between the rear of the cab and the high wooden rack. She let out a delighted woof and continued to bark as the truck headed up the dirt road.

Inside the cab, whirlwind Kayak turned around and around on the seat, trying to get her head out a window. Her long toenails dug into my jeans, and on one turn, she licked my father on the ear. Her fur still smelled from the skunk, and I pinched my nose.

"Ughh! I forgot that she stunk so bad!"

Fortunately, the wood wasn't too far away. Dad had cut down several trees a few weeks before, so we just needed to load it. As he parked the truck at the side of the road, Kayak exploded from the cab and Lady jumped from the back. Together, the two dogs investigated their surroundings, sniffing around bushes and logs.

Pulling on my heavy gloves, I followed Dad through the trees to where the wood lay. He tentatively lifted a log. "These are still kind of heavy. Can you lift them?"

I tried one and managed to get it into my arms.

"I'll get it," I said.

Effortlessly, Dad hoisted a log onto his shoulder and marched back toward the truck. I struggled to get a piece onto my shoulder, but lost hold and it tumbled to the ground. I lifted it again, and finally concluded it was easier just to carry it in my arms and sort of drag it. I trudged after my father.

We worked for quite a while without much conversation. After the truck was finally loaded, we heaped all the dead limbs into a pile in the center of a small clearing. That way, it would be less of a fire hazard. Later in the year, we could burn the piles without damaging surrounding trees.

Although it was hard work, I liked wood gathering—the smell of sawdust, the sound of the wood thumping into the truck, the knowledge that this back-breaking work would provide us with welcomed heat during the bitter winter months. I loved the sound of our feet scrush-scrushing through the low-growing Kinnikinnic bushes (they didn't have their red berries yet) and the Oregon grape plants with their loads of green "grapes."

Near the stack of logs, off to one side, stood a grove of white-trunked aspens. Their round, dainty leaves shivered in the slight breeze, and each leaf danced independently of the others.

Overhead, a flock of Canada geese flew steadily as they called to one another. "Ka-ronk! Ka-ronk!"

"Beautiful, aren't they?" Dad commented suddenly. He'd been looking, too.

The dogs raced by in a game of chase. Kayak leaped over a big, old log, leaving Lady alone on the other side. Lady barked in frustration, then dodged around the end just as Kayak vanished around the other end. Grateful that she'd come home after her moose escapade, I watched Kayak as she pranced.

"You know," I remarked, "It's funny how glad I am to have Kayak after I thought she might be lost forever."

My father smiled. "Sometimes that's the way it is," he agreed.

For a long moment, we both watched the geese high overhead. Then he added thoughtfully, "Sometimes we take things for granted until we almost lose them. We need to appreciate what we have—be grateful for family, for friends, for this beautiful world, for life."

Lady pushed against my legs, and I scratched her carefully behind the ears. Dad ran a finger across the old scar on his chin, as he often did when he was thinking.

"Do you think that almost dying in that car accident made you appreciate life more?" I asked. The accident had occurred in his senior year at college, before he married my mother.

"Oh, yes," he said. "And it made me ask questions about the meaning of life, too. I realized that it did matter whether or not there was a God out there, and I needed to find out why I was here. Sometimes it takes death to make us ask questions about life."

I seized upon the subject. "Is that how you became a Christian?"

"It was a start," he said. "It made me ask questions anyway. Then, after I married your mother, we had some rocky times, and it seemed that Christianity was the only hope for keeping our marriage together."

I had heard that story a lot. My parents had decided that they would really try Christianity wholeheartedly. They prayed for God to help them. Then they started studying the Bible, trying to do what it said. Over the years, God drew them closer to each other.

"It did work," Dad said simply. "We've seen God act in our lives in ways that weren't just coincidence or chance. For me, God allowed that accident—and then our marriage troubles—to get my attention. Then He used other life circumstances to prove Himself to me."

"Huh," I said.

"Not that God caused that pain," Dad continued. "But He uses those traumatic events in our lives to make us aware of Him, to bring something good out of even bad happenings."

I nodded, trying to sort out my conflicting thoughts. I was sure that God wouldn't want Deanna to challenge me as she had. Perhaps, though, God had used Deanna's question to get my attention. What exactly was He using to prove Himself to me?

Chapter 13: Not for My Birthday!

"Hand me those tongs, will you please?" With a hotpad, Mom lifted the lid off the water bath canner and a burst of steam rushed out, adding more heat to the already sweltering house. "Just a couple more minutes and these will be done."

"Sure, here!" I snatched the tongs from the table and quickly passed them over. Mom readjusted one of the jars in the boiling vat and clunked the lid back on, as I plopped onto a kitchen chair and wiped dampness from my face.

We'd been working together in the kitchen all morning, with the wood cookstove making the house way too warm. Next to the canner full of jars, a big pot of pickling syrup steamed on top of the stove, filling the air with the spicy smell of vinegar and cloves. Just as the syrup reached the boiling point, my mother began to scoop up handfuls of cucumber and onion slices, gradually stirring them into the mix. When the pan was full, she lifted it off the stove and set it on the counter.

"Want a bite?" Mom turned from the bubbling mix with a sample pickle in her spoon. I opened my mouth, and she popped in the warm, spicy slice. It tasted good, although the cucumber itself hadn't soaked up the spices much yet.

"Mmm," I said, opening my mouth for a second taste. I was chopping still more cucumbers for tomorrow's canning. They had to soak overnight in pickling salt before "graduating" to glass jars.

Although Penny had been gone almost a week, so far I had managed to pack that time full of things to do. Actually, my parents helped me with that! I unpacked more boxes, painted some new kitchen shelves, helped Dad haul and stack more firewood, and gave Kayak a few more baths in the creek. (She still smelled kind of bad.) I also spent lots of time helping Mom in the kitchen.

My mother always prepared for winter by canning boxes of fruits and vegetables that she and Dad brought home every time they drove to town. She reminded me of a squirrel, packing away nuts in its little hole. Sometimes, though, as my mother gleefully hauled another box of fresh fruit into the house, it seemed to me that the squirrel's job was easier! Squirrels didn't pit hundreds of thousands of tiny pie cherries before canning them. Squirrels didn't wash tomatoes until they were sick of them. Squirrels didn't slice giant piles of cucumbers to make into pickles! Although, even I had to admit, the squirrels would have a pretty bland diet all winter long. The hot hours over the stove would eventually be worth it. My mom's bread and butter pickles are the best pickles in the world.

"Won't it be lovely to have all these homemade pickles this winter?" Mom enthused, vigorously washing more canning jars. Before I could answer, she rapidly changed the subject. "Have you thought about what you'd like to do for your birthday?"

"Well," I said, carefully selecting another long, green cucumber to chop. "I wish we could watch a movie, but we can't."

My family had never been big TV or movie fans, but our birthdays had always been a chance to have at least one video. Without the TV, though, that seemed out of the question this year.

"Actually, we might be able to watch a movie," Mom said. "If the generator arrives in time, we can hook up a TV and VCR to that. I'll ask Dad about it."

"Really?" I said excitedly.

"*If* we can," Mom emphasized the *if*. "What would you like to see?"

I only needed a second to answer that one. "*Spirit of the Wind*," I said, remembering the dogsled movie that had inspired me at age five. "Do you think we can find it?"

"I don't know, we can look."

"And can Penny spend the night?"

"That sounds nice," Mom agreed. "Would you like Dixie and Deanna, too? A slumber party?"

Invite Dixie and Deanna to my birthday party? How had my mother come up with that one? I couldn't imagine anything worse. I shook my head, and then realized that Mom had her back to me.

"No," I said emphatically. "Just Penny." I swept the cucumber slices off the table into a clean, five-gallon bucket. Later we would mix in onions and peppers and salt; then the mixture would soak overnight until we canned them the next day.

"Okay." Mom gave a sigh of satisfaction as she dunked a clean jar in hot rinse water and carefully put it on the towel to dry. "Isn't that pretty in the sunlight?" She tipped her head and looked at it with a contented smile. "I'm sure we could manage to fit everyone if you do want a larger party."

"No thanks!"

My mother looked a little surprised at my vehement response. She raised a questioning eyebrow at me.

"Deanna doesn't believe in God," I explained, watching Mom closely to see her reaction. I wondered if she would say something like, "Well, then, I can see why you don't want her for your party." Of course, Mom didn't say anything of the sort. She didn't even look surprised.

"I'm not sure if her parents do either," Mom said. "So, I guess that's not surprising. Did she talk to you about it?" She moved the pan of hot pickles and syrup to the table and began setting clean jars nearby.

"Well, yeah," I said. "She told me that when they visited."

"They've had some difficult times lately, I think," Mom continued. "So Deanna may be kind of bitter."

I hadn't known that. I wondered what kind of trouble the Morrises had had? And how did Mom know?

"What kind of difficulties?" I asked.

"I'm don't really know." Mom took a soup ladle and began scooping the warm pickle mix into the hot clean jars. "Deanna's parents didn't say much, but it sounded as though they aren't really happy about their move up here. I'm sure that the girls could use friends. You know what it's like to be lonely."

Dismayed, I ran my fingers through the chopped cucumbers on the cutting board. Did that mean I had to invite them to my party?

"I think Dixie likes Patrick," I announced, hoping that would convince my mother not to throw a James/Ruffin/Morris slumber party. After all, my parents always told us never to date a non-Christian, because that could lead to a marriage that was "un-equally yoked." Surely Mom wouldn't want a non-Christian girl hanging around, trying to get Patrick's attention.

"Sounds normal." Mom's voice had an amused note. "She seems like a nice-enough girl. But I'm sure that Patrick will use his head."

"I don't think he even knows," I said.

"Hmm," Mom said. She didn't seem worried. "He might realize more than you think."

I strongly doubted that, but, then again, you never could know about Patrick. Just as I gave up all hope for a quiet, thirteenth birthday, Mom added, "Of course you don't have to invite them if you don't want to. It's your birthday. Maybe we can have them up for a visit another time."

I relaxed with a sigh of relief. Saved!

"Just think about what I've said," Mom added.

Suddenly the front door was flung open and Patrick stuck his head in. "Mom? Can you come here a second? I need to ask you about something." Out of the corner of my eye, I saw him give a mysterious nod toward me. Another birthday secret?

"I'll come, too," I volunteered, as a sudden teasing spirit caught me. "I need to get out of this hot kitchen."

Patrick looked dismayed, probably wondering how to fend me off without giving away that he had a secret. I took advantage of the moment to dry my hands on a towel, acting as if I really were coming.

"I think you'd better stay, Jess," Mom said, having mercy on my brother. "Tis the season for secrets!"

I don't know where she'd come up with that line, but we always used it when we were planning surprises, especially birthday or Christmas gifts. Now I knew for sure that something was up!

Mom and Patrick left me to the canning. I just kept quietly scooping warm pickles and vinegar into the clean jars, wondering what my family was planning. Patrick was a good carpenter, so he might be making anything from a simple bookshelf to a window-seat for my loft. I favored the window-seat idea, actually—especially if it had a trunk with a lid. I could make little pillows to match my curtains. Should they be checked, or flowered, or some solid color? No matter what I used, it would have to include blue, my favorite color.

Thump!

The sudden noise startled me, and I looked up from the pickles with a jump. Something rustled again, behind me. I turned cautiously, peeking over my shoulder. Something under the counter moved again, imperceptibly, but I couldn't make out what it was. With a bit of a shudder, I turned around completely, the ladle of hot pickles in my hand.

A patch of grayish fur flashed under the counter again, and suddenly I saw it—an ugly creature, bigger than a squirrel, with a furry tail and bright, beady, black eyes. Just a few feet away, the animal moved toward me across the floor—slowly, in sudden jerks, like some monstrous, battery-operated, stuffed animal.

Chapter 14: Pickles and Packrat

With a wild scream, I hurled the ladle of hot pickles at the approaching animal and scrambled onto a kitchen chair. The ladle crashed to the floor as the creature dodged away and vanished behind the counter in a shower of warm, sticky pickle chips.

"Jessica? Are you all right?" Mom flung open the cabin door. Dad and Patrick peered in right behind her. They must have all been standing on the porch. "Did you get burned?" My mother cast an anxious glance at the hot stove and boiling water bath canner.

I stared at the pickle puddle spreading across the plywood floor and shuddered. Then I shuddered again. "There was an animal, like a squirrel—" I tried to explain with my hands.

Patrick got wildly excited. "It sounds like a packrat! Where'd it go?" he asked. "Let's pull the counter away from the wall!"

"Be careful," Mom warned.

"Here, let's call Kayak," Dad said. "She's the rat hunter. Kayak! Come here!"

So that was one of the mysterious packrats that Penny had told me about. Somehow I'd expected it to look different.

"Here, Patrick, pull the counter this way." Dad opened the cabin door and Kayak bounced eagerly inside. "Jessica, can you give him a hand?"

Gingerly, I climbed down from my chair. I was not at all comfortable with the idea of trying to find the rat again, but I joined the rest of the family. Mom, Patrick, and I pulled the heavy kitchen counter away from the log wall, while Dad and Kayak stood guard at the end by the door, peering into the dark crack between the counter and wall. Kayak certainly looked interested, with her eyes bright and ears perked. It didn't work as planned, though.

First of all, the counter was hard to pull. When it finally did slide out a few more inches, the rat scrambled out right under my feet, instead of at Kayak's end. As I jumped away, I slipped on the spilled pickles and sprawled onto the sticky, kitchen floor. The rat ran under the stove, behind the woodpile, and around the garbage can before it turned in confusion and ran straight back toward me. Kayak pounced at it, but I was in her way and couldn't move in time.

"Look out!" Mom yelled.

I screamed.

For a second, everything became a confused blur of gray rat fur, Kayak's black fur, and assorted legs. A moment later, I found myself standing on the kitchen chair again, looking at the puzzled faces of my parents and brother. Kayak, just as confused, investigated behind the cream-and-green cookstove and the wooden counter. The rat had vanished.

"Where'd it go?" Patrick asked the obvious question.

We held our breaths and listened again. The room was silent except for Kayak's eager panting. On the porch, Lady gave an anxious bark. She hated being left out of the excitement. At that moment, though, I would have gladly traded places with her!

"Where did it come from?" I shuddered.

All of a sudden, Kayak pounced toward the woodpile and the rat scrambled out, right between the wolf-dog's front paws. Scooting between Kayak's back legs, the rat raced into the living room and disappeared again.

"Okay." My father took command. "Patrick, open the back door. I'll open the front, and we'll let both dogs look. Maybe they'll at least chase it outside."

No sooner said than done. We let Lady in, and she and Kayak scouted out the living room, lower bedroom, office, and washroom. Nothing stirred. Dad climbed up and checked out the loft bedrooms. Although we poked around in dark corners for about twenty minutes, we finally gave up without seeing even another rat whisker, much to Kayak's disappointment—not to mention mine. I shuddered at the thought of waking up with a rat in my bedroom!

Dad borrowed a box trap from the Ruffins—it looked like a metal cage with a sliding trap door on one end—and set it up behind the kitchen stove. He suspected that the rat had crept inside the cabin some night when the back door had been open. I wondered if it had a nest in our house somewhere.

"Wouldn't it work to bait the trap with aluminum foil?" I asked, watching Dad spread peanut butter on an apple slice to set inside the box.

"Aluminum foil? Why?" Dad sounded puzzled.

"Well, Penny said that packrats like to trade things for something shiny."

"I've heard that, too." He snugged the box against the wall. "I'd guess that they would choose food over aesthetics, though."

"Do they really trade stuff?"

"Actually, they don't really *trade*," my father explained, tugging the counter back into place beneath the kitchen window. "Apparently they just like collecting things for their nests, and they often carry around little items they find. But, when they find something that they want more, they drop whatever it was that they had and pick up the new thing. I guess that's why they're called pack-rats. That's just a nickname for the bushytail woodrat, actually."

"Huh," I mused. I sure had a story to tell Penny!

After my father set up the trap, and after we scrubbed all the smashed pickles and vinegar off the floor, Mom and I returned to our canning—and to the topic of the Morrises and the Big Question.

"Why do I believe in God?" My mother slowly swished the dishcloth around in the water. "What makes you ask that?"

"Deanna asked me."

"She asked you why I believed in God?"

"No, why *I* believed." I chopped down a little harder than necessary on an offending cucumber, sending a small chunk flying onto the floor. "And then I was talking to Dad about how God uses events in our lives to show Himself to us. Was there something special in your life?"

She thought for a moment. "Well," she said finally, "When I was little, we used to hear Bible stories in church. I always wished there was a God like the Bible talked about, a God Who really cared about people. But I didn't think there was…and they didn't tell us that in church, oddly enough. Our church was more of a social place to go—rather than a place to learn truth."

She picked up a pair of goose potholders and carefully carried another heavy container of hot pickles to the table so we could ladle them into the clean jars. We began the hot job of transferring the pickles, spoonful by spoonful.

"I went to a Christian college for a couple years," she continued. "And I met people there that were different—people who seemed to really know something about God. And for the first time, I heard that the Bible was true, not just old stories. My friends seemed to have a peace and purpose for living that I didn't have. I wanted what they had."

"What did you do?" I plopped another ladle of pickles into a new jar, being careful not to spill any. They were still hot.

"I finally got desperate," Mom said. "I just went into the chapel one night and knelt down and asked God if He were there to please show me. And He did. An incredible peace just overflowed me and I knew."

"That's all?" I asked.

"Well, for me, that was a start," Mom said. "That's what I needed. Over time, as I continued to pray and read Scripture, I started to see more evidences of God. Now it's so clear to me—but you can't always start with everything figured out."

"Dad told me that a lot happened after you got married," I said, recalling the conversation when my father and I hauled firewood.

"It did," Mom agreed. "Although I believed in God in college, I still had an awful lot to learn. Your father and I really struggled for the first few years of our marriage, until we both decided to commit ourselves to the Lord wholeheartedly. Until then, we couldn't agree on things; we couldn't forgive each other; we both struggled with pride. The Lord helped us to change those things."

We worked in silence for a moment. Then she continued, "I think we would have gotten divorced if we hadn't turned to God instead. We loved each other, but we didn't have ways to work things out. God gave us wisdom to solve our problems and perseverance to stay together. He also gave us peace, because we learned that He had a plan for our lives."

"Huh." I frowned. The unanswered questions still nagged at me, but I had begun to hope that I could find real answers. It was like solving a mystery, putting clue and clue together, hoping to crack the big case— the case for the existence of God.

Crash! Something gave a metallic clang behind the hot stove, and an animal yowled in sudden fright. We could hear the rattling of the box trap against the wall and woodpile.

"The trap!" Mom exclaimed, dropping her ladle into the pickle mix. "Call your dad!"

Chapter 15: Attacked

I hesitated. The noise didn't sound exactly like a packrat. Instead of running out to call my father, I hastily dropped to my knees and peered underneath the stove. Sure enough, the trap held a small animal—a small, cream-colored creature with a black face, black tail, and frightened blue eyes.

"Yaowraohhw! Yaowraohhw!"

"Oh, no!" I exclaimed. "It's Parka!"

"Oh, dear!" Mom echoed. "We should have thought…"

We scrambled to pull out the cage and open the trap door on the end. Fortunately, my Siamese had managed to pull her entire, long, black tail into the box with her. Although a tight squeeze, she didn't appear injured at all—just frightened. She raced up the stairs into my loft with her tail puffy, and I didn't see her the rest of the afternoon.

"I think I've had all the excitement I can handle for one day," Mom sighed. "I hope nothing else happens."

It didn't. At least nothing alarming. We just canned pickles, pickles, and more pickles all afternoon.

***

On Monday, Penny returned, sunburned and happy. She bounced into the house around two o'clock, spilling over with stories about camp.

"You'll never guess," she started off. "I learned how to swim!"

"You did?" I said.

"Yes, Kristin—she was our counselor—showed me how. She kept holding onto me until I could float on my own. Kristin's a lifeguard when she's not a counselor, so she wasn't a lifeguard at camp." Penny paused for breath. "Except she sort of lifeguarded when she was showing me how to swim—and I think I'm going to be a lifeguard someday, but I need to learn to swim better first."

"Did you see any Sasquatches?" I teased.

Penny laughed. "Not this year! Not even any bears! But this was still the best-ever year! See what we made in the craft shop?"

She un-tucked her T-shirt and held out the front so I could read it. All the girls in her cabin—plus about ten other people, including the minister—had written their names on the front and back, along with addresses and comments like "Don't forget the mustard!" and "Roses are red, violets are blue, I don't snore but you sure do!"

"I got almost everybody that I knew," Penny said. "But Kari left before I got her, so I might mail the shirt to her so she can sign it, too, but I'm not sure if she'll send it back. Kari forgets stuff."

Scarcely pausing for breath, Penny continued on with stories of Kristin, the other five girls in her little cabin, campfires in the evenings, fireworks over the water, nature hikes, and chapel outside in the early mornings, as the mist rose from the lake behind the pulpit.

My mother, trying to balance her checkbook at the kitchen table, looked up from her calculator after about ten minutes and suggested that we pack a lunch and go for a picnic.

"What shall we take?" I asked.

"Tuna sandwiches, chips, and lemonade," Mom said. "There might be a couple of cookies left, too."

Penny volunteered to make the lemonade, so I found her a big glass jar. She worked happily away, mixing the sugar and dipping water from our five-gallon water buckets. I made the sandwiches—nice juicy ones with pickles and mayonnaise. I love tuna. I don't think I'll ever eat enough of it.

"Do you want a sandwich, Mom?" I asked.

"Sure!" She looked up briefly and smiled at me.

"We put on skits on the last night," Penny continued. "Our cabin did Noah's ark, and I was the zebra. I made ears out of construction paper to put on my hat with pins. Then we built a campfire and roasted marshmallows and made S'mores."

"Did you tell ghost stories?" I asked, remembering our conversation by the river.

"Not *ghost* stories," Penny explained. "We told scary stories, but not *ghost* stories. Kristin says that there aren't really ghosts. Sometimes people think they see them because Satan is playing tricks. She said we don't have to be afraid of ghosts because God is stronger than Satan."

I thought that sounded right. No argument on that point!

"So," Penny said, "It wasn't any use telling ghost stories any more because they aren't really scary." She shrugged her shoulders, as if to dismiss all ghosts.

I'd never thought of that before. Then again, my parents hadn't let us tell ghost stories. Occasionally Patrick would try to scare me with a story about a bear. When I was little, I was scared to death that the abominable snowman would come after me—something that Patrick used to his advantage! After we read *The Hobbit*, I had a nagging suspicion that that strange creature, Gollum, lived in our pantry. I could hardly bear to pass the dark pantry doorway, even though my mind knew it couldn't possibly be true. Anyway, I guess it was good that Patrick hadn't been allowed to tell me ghost stories!

"There." Penny poured the lemonade into the thermos bottles and tightened the caps. "Let's go!"

We collected our lunch, waved goodbye to my mother, and set off up the hill toward the treehouse, just about three hundred yards away. Since it was such a close walk and I wouldn't be able to watch her very well from the treehouse, I left Kayak behind, tied to a pine near the cabin. She howled as we left, as only a lonely wolf-pup can howl. It was heartbreaking.

"We'll be back soon," I called to the dismayed dog.

"Why can't you bring her along?" Penny asked. "Poor puppy."

"I can't," I said. "Something knocked over the garbage three times this week. I have to keep her tied unless I'm watching her."

"Was it her that knocked it over?" my friend asked, in sudden perception.

"I don't know. I don't see how it could have been, but Patrick keeps saying it wasn't Lady, either."

"Maybe it was the Sasquatch we saw in the woods." Penny shivered.

"We didn't actually see it," I reminded her.

"Yeah," Penny admitted, unconvinced. "But…"

A few minutes later we reached the treehouse ladder and climbed up, pushing open the trap door overhead. Once inside, we plopped the door down again to "lock" it. There was a piece of wood nailed to the floor that twisted around to hold the door down tightly. It wasn't actually made for a lock. It was made to keep the door flat, so that the edge didn't stick up and trip people. It worked okay for a lock, though.

"Guess what I saw while you were gone?"

"What?" Penny looked up from opening the lunch bag.

"A packrat!" I said.

"No way!"

I nodded. "Yes, he came into our kitchen when I was canning pickles. He came out from under the counter and almost ran right over me."

"Did you catch him?" Penny asked, wide-eyed. I had a sudden vision of swooping the grotesque, furry animal into my arms. I shook my head.

"Oh, wow!" Penny said. "Maybe he'll leave you something." She seemed to regard the creature as some kind of wild tooth fairy.

"I don't know," I said. To tell the truth, I didn't ever want to see a packrat again, much less have him creep into my room after dark! "We set a box trap, so maybe that will get him."

Penny, who seemed set on the idea, suggested that I could leave little balls of aluminum foil on my bedroom floor so that the rat would trade me something for them. "Maybe even a watch," she said, then amended hastily, "An antique one."

"It wouldn't matter if it was an antique or not," I said. "It still would have to come *from* somebody. And if it did leave a watch, I'd have to find out who lost it. Rats don't just own watches."

Penny laughed. "Can you imagine if they did have watches?" she said. "How would they wear them?" She checked an imaginary watch on her wrist and wrinkled up her nose, pretending to be a rat. "Well, well, time to build a nest. Let's see if we can steal some socks for a warm bed."

I giggled. Penny looked as much like a packrat as a person could— especially for never having seen one herself. Getting into the mood of the moment, I put my hands in front of me, curled over like huge paws and jerked toward Penny to demonstrate how it moved. She shrieked and jumped back, sitting on a sandwich and spilling her lemonade.

"Yeek! Oh no!"

We scrambled to clean it up, and I was just ready to open the trap-door and throw out a dirty sandwich when I heard a sudden thump.

"Penny! Listen!"

"What?"

We both fell quiet. In the brief silence that followed, I heard it. Outside the treehouse, below us, something made a woofing sound. Penny and I both froze, wide-eyed.

Something bumped the trap door. The whole treehouse shivered slightly.

"Is it a dog?" Penny whispered.

I managed to shake my head no. Whatever it was had to be bigger than a dog if it could touch the treehouse. The trapdoor wiggled again, but the little block of wood held it for the moment. Something scratched the floor beneath us.

"Let's look," Penny whispered. Trembling, we crept to the window. Just below us, half-hidden by the floor of the treehouse, we saw the furry black back of an animal standing on its hind legs.

"It's a bear!" I squeaked.

"Bigfoot!" Penny shrieked at the same time.

We jumped back from the window. The treehouse shook again, and the trapdoor wiggled.

"Quick!" Penny yelled in a whisper. "Move the table over the door to hold it down!"

We slid the heavy, wooden box-table onto the door and then stacked the bookshelf on top of that.

"What can we do?" I quavered, envisioning the creature climbing after us. I wasn't sure that even the heavy table could keep it out of the treehouse.

Penny's eyes were round with fear. "He might break the windows."

Fortunately the windows were nearly seven feet off the ground. The bear looked shorter than that because he had to stand on his hind feet to touch the floor of the treehouse. Could he climb the trees?

"The tuna!" I said. "Maybe he smells the fish!"

"Are there any sandwiches left?" Penny scrambled through the lunch bag, looking. "Here's two. Let's throw them out the window!"

One of the windows actually opened by sliding upwards, so we cautiously pushed it up just enough for Penny to toss the sandwiches out. They bounced off the bear's back, and he turned around to sniff them.

I held my breath.

Chapter 16: The Trap

The bear gulped down the sandwiches, then ambled back toward the treehouse and stood up on its hind legs again. A scratching sound came through the floorboards and we felt another bump. Penny and I clutched each other.

"Do you think he knows we're in here?" Penny whispered, her eyes round with terror.

"I don't know," I quavered. "But it doesn't matter if he knows or not. We *are* here."

"We're going to have to scream," Penny said, her voice gaining confidence. "Then Daddy will come."

A suggestion was all it took. We each gulped a deep breath and started yelling, nearly deafening each other as the sound bounced off the walls of the tiny room. Then Penny remembered the emergency whistle that she always wore around her neck, and she started blowing it, too.

When the screaming began, the bear lumbered away from the treehouse and headed for the woods. Just as it disappeared, I saw my father break through the grove of aspens. He was running faster than I'd ever seen him run in my entire life—even faster than when our church was playing softball, and he hit a home run. Patrick, normally a really fast runner, panted at his heels, barely keeping up, and Lady was behind them.

"Jessica? Jessica!" Dad bellowed, just as I heard someone from the other direction yelling, "Penny?" It was her father, running from his house.

"We're here!" we shrieked, flinging open the window all the way and leaning out. "There goes the bear!"

"Where? A bear? Are you okay?"

Well, after our frightened explanations, our fathers seemed both upset and relieved at the same time.

"Something must be wrong with it," Dad said. "It shouldn't have come so close to the houses. Usually, they are shyer than that."

"We've never seen any this near," Mr. Ruffin said, holding Penny tightly. "And we've been here ten years."

"Let's follow it," Patrick suggested, disappointed that he'd missed all the action. "Which way did it go?"

Dad shook his head. "What would we do when we found it? It's not the season for hunting bear, so we can't shoot it without landing a huge fine. It probably was attracted to the tuna."

"Besides, it's probably far away by now," Penny's father agreed. "When you yelled, it must have been pretty scared. We aren't going to find it now."

"It really ran," I said, still shaking, and casting nervous glances toward the trees.

"If it's sick or something," Dad said, "It may be back. We'd better call the Forest Service and see about getting a trap set."

Penny started to cry. "I want to go home!" she wailed.

I felt the same way, but I managed to keep from crying. I just leaned up against Dad and rubbed Lady's gray ears.

"I'm going into town this afternoon," Mr. Ruffin said. "Why don't I call the Department of Fish and Game and see if they'll set a trap?"

"That's a good idea," Dad agreed. "Meanwhile, I guess you girls better stay closer to the house."

After that, the Ruffins went home, Penny still crying. Dad, Patrick, and I walked back to our house, going over the details all over again. Patrick thought we should set a bear trap ourselves. He had a variety of suggestions about how we could build a big cage, but my father didn't seem to think any of the ideas were wise.

"I don't think we'll mess with it," he said. "If Fish and Game catch it, so much the better."

"Do you think that's what I heard by the river when I went fishing with Penny?" I asked, remembering the crack in the bushes.

"Well," Dad said. "It might have been. I am just glad that treehouse is halfway sturdy."

"Me, too!" I nodded vigorously. "But I don't think it would have held up if the bear really wanted to get in."

"Possibly not." Dad shook his head again. "I can't believe it would come so close. You were practically within sight of the house!" He seemed almost as shaken as I was. "With all the activity around here, and the dogs, the vehicles driving around…I had no idea a bear would dare to come in this close." His voice trailed off again.

"You didn't even grab a gun," Patrick said.

"There wasn't time," Dad said. "I thought if I stopped to get a rifle Jessica would be—" He stopped, as if his thoughts were too awful to speak.

"When you heard us screaming, did you know it was a bear?" I asked.

"I didn't know." Dad shook his head again, and reached over to put his arm around my shoulders. "But your screaming was awful—it sounded like you were being mauled to death."

I suddenly realized that, if he'd discovered the bear actually attacking Penny and me, my father would have jumped right in the middle of it, bare-handed, with no thought for himself. Unable to speak for a moment, I finally choked out, "Thanks, Dad." It didn't seem like enough, but I didn't know what else to say.

When we entered the house, we discovered my mother placidly chopping more cucumbers in the kitchen, singing along with the radio. She hadn't heard a thing—not even our screaming.

As we told her about the bear, her eyes grew huge and she gave me a long hug. "Thank the Lord you are both okay," she said quietly.

Dad told her that the Ruffins were going to contact the Department of Fish and Game about setting a bear trap. Then both Mom and Dad suggested—actually ordered might be a better word—that I stay right by the cabin for the next few days. I certainly didn't need to be told that! Suddenly, I thought of lots of things that I could do in the house. There were books I hadn't read, letters I hadn't written…

I curled up on the couch all afternoon, and was quickly absorbed by my latest copy of *Sled!*, the Alaskan dogsled magazine that my parents had ordered for me for Christmas. It featured interviews with famous dogsledders, articles about dog-training, and ads for anything from dog harnesses to used dogsleds. I always checked the dogsled ads, vainly hoping that someone in northwestern Montana would sell one in my price range, within a hundred dollars or so. So far, all the prices were sky-high—and most of the sleds were in Alaska!

That night, I dreamed about bears and woke up in alarm when the dogs began to bark downstairs. Although I was certain that I'd felt the soft brush of bear fur, all I found was Parka, curled cozily on my chest and purring. I stroked her silky fur while I consciously tried to slow my breathing.

"Kayak, be quiet!" Patrick ordered crossly from his loft. "Lady, hush!"

Both dogs quieted, although Kayak growled a few more times.

I repeated Psalm 23 to myself about six times before I fell asleep again. Somehow, it was always comforting.

The Lord is my shepherd, I shall not want. He makes me lie down in green pastures; He leads me beside quiet waters. He restores my soul…Even though I walk through the valley of the shadow of death, I fear no evil; for Thou art with me.

This time, I dreamed about Kayak, running joyously through the wind, her tail waving. I dreamed about two moose with long Roman noses. I dreamed about Penny with St. Peter on her shoulder. Then Patrick laughed and jumped into the creek, splashing water at me.

Startled, I woke up to find Lady on my bed, licking me with her wet tongue. Patrick was laughing at my door.

"Lady, stop!" I sputtered as the dog earnestly and gently licked my cheek, intent on her mission of kindness. "Patrick, how'd you get her up here?"

"Just carried her," he said. "Mom said to get you up."

"I'm up! I'm up!" I exclaimed. "Lady, go away!"

"Come on, Lady," Patrick said. "Let's see if we can get you down from here."

It turned out to be harder than expected. Not only was the Australian shepherd heavy, but she was also scared of heights. She would barely come within reach of Patrick's outstretched arm. When he finally grabbed her, she tried to dig her claws into the boards as he pulled her across the floor.

"Come here," he puffed.

Finally, I crawled out of bed and pushed the dog while Patrick pulled with one hand and tried to get his arm around her, while he was still hanging onto the ladder. Somehow we managed to get the terrified dog back to solid ground, but I doubted Patrick would ever try that again.

The dogs had both slept in the house that night, so I was surprised when I went outside to see trash scattered all over the yard again. I walked over and righted the can, looking around curiously. There was a big patch of soft earth nearby where we always dumped dishwater, and I noticed tracks in it. They were almost human tracks—except for the claw prints.

Two seconds later I found myself inside. "There are bear tracks by the garbage can!" I gasped. "That's what's been knocking over the trash at night!"

They *were* bear tracks. My father shook his head grimly when he saw them, and drove to town to make a second report about the bear. Later that afternoon, a biologist and game warden showed up from the Department of Fish and Game. They were driving a big green truck. Most importantly, they towed a bear trap behind the truck.

The trap was made of what looked like big pipes, bent into a flat-bottomed tunnel with a curved roof, painted yellow. It was about ten feet long with a big wheel on each side, so that it could be pulled. On one end, a sliding gate dropped down to close it.

The rangers pulled the trap near the edge of the trees between the cabin and the treehouse, unhitched it from the truck, and baited it with rotten meat. They fastened the door so it would stay open until the bear went inside the cage and pulled on the meat. Then the door would crash down to trap the animal inside.

"I don't think it'll work." Penny stood with her hands on her hips, as we watched from the porch. She had driven down with her father. "I wouldn't be dumb enough to walk into that thing. I don't see why any old bear would either!"

I saw her point, but I thought it might work—especially if they used tunafish for bait! I didn't suggest the idea though.

Now, all we had to do was wait.

Chapter 17: Patrick's Secret

Well, we waited.

And waited.

And waited.

The bear trap stood silent and empty, and nothing disturbed our garbage can for the rest of the week. Penny and I spent those long days inside either my cabin or hers, not only because of the bear but because of a miserable, gray rain that came and went. The dogs huddled in their doghouses or came into the cabin to dry off their smelly coats. Parka curled up on my bed and slept for hours, and St. Peter huddled miserably in a tree, with his head under a shiny, black wing. Penny and I played checkers until we could see black and red circles every time we closed our eyes.

Patrick stayed hidden in his woodshop, and my father spent a lot of time out there, too. Although I often wondered what they were building, I managed to wait patiently. I knew I could hang on for a few more days until my birthday. When he wasn't with Patrick, Dad was wiring up fluorescent lights and a CB in our house, to run off the batteries that he charged with the generator that had finally arrived.

After several drizzly days, though, the morning of my thirteenth birthday dawned bright and clear. When I woke up, it seemed as if all the birds in the whole world were singing their hearts out just outside my window. The sunlight streamed in as I lay under my patchwork quilt, wiggling my right foot.

Parka, eyes closed, lay like a heavy weight right in the middle of the bed, purring softly. She took up a lot of space for a small cat, squashing me to one side. I pushed her a bit with my knees, but she didn't even stir.

I could hear whispered conversation downstairs. The front door opened and closed, and Patrick said distinctly, "We're ready."

Mom's quieter voice made a reply that I couldn't make out. Then Dad called out, "Jessica? Are you up?"

His voice died down, as my mother interjected something about letting me sleep in. Before they had time to debate the issue further, I rolled out of bed eagerly, thumping my bare feet on the board floor. Parka hopped off my bed in a huff and stalked out the door onto the landing. I heard her claws scratching on the ladder as she climbed down.

"Just a minute!" I sang out.

"I wish she'd get up that fast every morning!" Dad said, and I heard Mom's soft laughter.

Quickly I scrambled into blue jeans and a red T-shirt before climbing down.

"Happy Birthday!" My family said together as I emerged. They were all standing in the kitchen, waiting for me with smiles on their faces. Kayak, finally dry and wearing a red ribbon around her neck, came over to press her nose into my hand, and Lady wagged her tail.

I beamed back at everybody, noticing the little pile of wrapped presents on the table next to my plate, and the blue and white streamers decorating my chair. After everybody hugged me, we all gathered at the table with cups of hot cocoa (a birthday tradition, even in the middle of summer).

The first three packages were looped together with a curious arrangement of white yarn tied tightly around all the corners. I recognized this as Mom's handiwork and looked to her for an explanation.

She laughed. "Open the flat one first."

With much use of the scissors, I untangled the biggest package and slit open the blue tissue paper. The gift was an orange booklet, stapled together along the edge. I turned it over to see the cover: *How to Make Your Own Dog Racing Harness.*

With a squeal of delight, I jumped up to give Mom another hug. Now I could start training Kayak to pull a sled! "Where'd you get it?" I asked excitedly.

She smiled. "We had to special-order it from the bookstore," she told me. "It was hard to find, but it seems like it has good directions for any size dog."

I carefully laid the book on the table and eagerly opened the smallest package. It contained a big, heavy-duty needle, a roll of waxed cord, a small metal ring, and a piece of soft, brown, fake fur.

"The cord is to stitch the harness with," Dad explained. "That will probably be sturdier than ordinary thread."

"Or you can sew with dental floss," Patrick volunteered. "I can save mine for you."

I rolled my eyes at my brother. "Thanks so much. I'd *love* to sew with your old dental floss."

He laughed.

"The fur is to pad the harness with, on the chest and neck pieces," Mom said, "so that Kayak won't chafe her skin."

"And the ring?"

"That's to put at the back of the harness, to snap on to the line from the sled." Dad finished off his hot cocoa and set the cup down on the table.

As I guessed, the last package contained a roll of one-inch wide, blue, nylon webbing for making the harness. It looked kind of like unpadded backpack straps.

"That's four yards," Mom said. "According to the book, it's enough for one dog harness. If you don't like the color, we can exchange it for either pink or black."

"Oh, I like it," I said hastily. "Blue is great!" I could already picture Kayak, fitted with the beautiful blue harness, pulling me over the snow. Eagerly, I opened the little book again. It had lots of pictures and diagrams showing how to measure the dog so that the harness pieces could be cut to the right lengths, how to fasten the fake fur on as padding, and how to stitch the pieces together with the waxed thread. I could hardly wait to start.

"This will be wonderful!" I beamed. My parents looked glad. I expected that they had spent a long time getting all the pieces together.

"Are you going to open the rest?" Patrick asked impatiently.

"The rest" turned out to be a book of Sherlock Holmes stories and three big chocolate bars without almonds. I was delighted. I just love to spend a whole afternoon reading a new book and eating chocolate, and this seemed like a splendid birthday. There seemed to be something missing, though. What had Patrick been making in the shop?

Puzzled, I looked at my brother, but before I could open my mouth, he suggested, "Why don't you look outside?"

When I started for the front door, Patrick nearly knocked me over in his eagerness to open it. Mom and Dad were both right behind me as I stepped onto the porch, Kayak and Lady at my heels.

There ahead of the steps, in a patch of golden sunlight, stood a long sled with skis for runners. The sled had side rails that swooped up from the round front to meet a curved handlebar at the back, about three feet off the ground.

A dogsled.

Chapter 18: In the Night

Stunned, I stood in silence for a moment, unable to believe my eyes. A dogsled? Could Patrick really have built a dogsled? Then I realized that three pairs of eyes were watching me anxiously.

"Do you like it?" Patrick asked.

His question broke the spell. The tears that had threatened to come disappeared as I turned to throw my arms around my brother and my dad. "Thank you! Thank you!" I choked. "Where...How did you..."

Patrick laughed. "It's from Dad, too." he said.

"What do you mean 'where' and 'how'?" Dad teased, looking pleased as I hugged him. "It didn't just pop into being!"

"I know!" I said. "I just never expected you to build one!"

I rushed forward to look more closely. Dad and Patrick went over it with me, describing every detail and explaining how they had worked on the sled since before our move to Steller's Creek.

"You've been wanting to sled for so long," Mom interjected. "And now with all these old logging roads around here, and since you have Kayak, we thought that you should have a proper sled."

"We wanted to buy one," Patrick said, "but they cost a lot of money."

"I know it! This is wonderful!" I ran my hand over the smooth, oak slats that made the bottom of the seat or "basket." Those pieces were varnished, but the rest of the sled wasn't.

"We had quite a time bending those skis up in the front," Dad said. "We had to steam them for quite a while, but they seem to be holding up just fine. They're a bit wider than a normal racing sled."

"We cut all the wood pieces before we left Kalispell," Patrick said, "but we didn't put them together until we finally got here." He groaned. "We had a tough time getting it up here without you seeing it."

"So that's why you wouldn't let me into your shop!"

Kayak sniffed with interest around the sled. She especially seemed intrigued by the little pieces of leather-looking strips that had been tied around many of the sled joints.

"That's rawhide." Patrick saw me looking at the leather pieces. "We tied it on the sled wet, and it tightened up as it dried. That way, the joints are more flexible than if we used bolts. Watch out that Kayak doesn't chew it off. She already ate a piece that we had in the shop."

"Wow." I still could hardly speak for amazement.

"Try standing on the runners." Dad gestured toward the back, where the skis extended behind the basket for a couple of feet. Some pieces of black bicycle tire tread had been nailed on top of the runners, so that it would be less slippery where my feet rested.

"So that's what you used that old bike tire for!" I remembered Patrick taking apart the tire on the day of our big argument.

I took hold of the handlebar and stepped onto the runners, feeling the roughness of the tire rubber catch the soles of my sandals. Down the middle of the sled, beneath the basket, ran the brake board. It hinged at the front of the sled, and the other end had a metal claw attached. Tentatively, I stepped on it, feeling the claw bite into the gray earth. In the winter, the brake board would help slow the sled.

"It's not the exact size of a normal racing sled," Dad said. "But we figured it would work for training Kayak."

"It's wonderful!" I almost felt like I was going to cry for joy.

"Did you see the designs on the back?" Mom had just been standing there, looking pleased at my delight.

Looking closely at the supports in the back (called stanchions), I discovered that little figures had been burned into the wood. The design was a team of four dogs, pulling a sled that had a tiny person balanced on the back of the runners. There was no mistaking who had done the wood-burning; they were so unmistakably Patrick's work that I laughed.

"That took a long time," Patrick informed me with a grin.

I ran my fingers over the handlebar again. I could almost hear the swish of runners and feel the wind in my face as I imagined Kayak, proudly wearing her new blue harness, pulling me through the blinding snow.

After completely inspecting my wonderful new sled, I spent the rest of my birthday morning starting to make the new harness. I had to wash the webbing and let it dry, just in case it would shrink. Then I measured the wiggly Kayak, trying to figure out how wide to make the neck loop and how long to make the straps that ran from her chest to her tail. In the afternoon, I lay on the couch, read some of the Sherlock Holmes stories, and nibbled on the candy. By the time Penny came down for pizza and chocolate cake with us, I felt very relaxed.

After dinner, Dad hooked up our VCR to the new generator, and we watched *Spirit of the Wind* and ate popcorn. Then Penny stayed overnight, so we giggled and talked until almost three in the morning. The day was so packed with different things that we hardly paid any attention to the still-empty yellow bear cage at the edge of the trees. We still had to keep Kayak and Lady in the house or tied up so they wouldn't go into the trap. That old rotten bait smelled wonderful to them.

After the excitement of the birthday, I didn't sleep too well. Penny finally dozed off in the middle of a conversation, but I guess I'd eaten too much chocolate. Anyway, it took a long time to get to sleep. I thought about my new sled until I dreamed about it, and then I had nightmares about the bear attacking us. I woke up all scared in the middle of the night and lay there in the dark with my heart thumping.

The white light from a full moon spilled into the window, casting great shadows on the walls. Once I thought I saw something move. I stared with wide eyes, but the shadow didn't stir again. I stole a peak at Penny, but my friend slept blissfully on, oblivious to any menaces from the dark. I took a deep breath, closed my eyes again, and tried to pray Psalm 23 to myself.

"The Lord is my shepherd, I shall not want," I whispered. "Even though I walk through the valley of the shadow of death, I fear no evil; for Thou art with me."

Tonight even Psalm 23 didn't help. It just made me think about Deanna's question again. Was there a God? Mom and Dad both seemed sure there was. Dad said that he believed in God partly because things happened in his life that didn't seem to be just accidents. My mother, on the other hand, seemed to have actually *felt* God's presence somehow. Knowing my practical mother, I was certain that she probably had. She wasn't the kind of person to imagine things.

Now, if Penny had "felt" God like Mom had, I might have wondered if she'd imagined it. Even so, Penny didn't imagine *everything*. Just because she imagined a lot of things didn't mean that *nothing* she said was true. So, even if Penny told me that she'd felt like God was there, it could have been true, too. My mother was especially believable, though.

I rolled over in bed, thumping my pillow and trying to get comfortable enough to sleep. Penny sighed once, but didn't wake up. The room darkened, then lightened again as the moon slipped between clouds.

I remembered something else Mom had said during our canning. She told me that reading the Bible and praying for many years had helped her to see more evidences for the existence of God. Mom said I couldn't always start with everything all figured out. Dad said that it took him a lot of time to grow more convinced about God.

I sighed, suddenly feeling a bit drowsier. All these thoughts seemed to be pulling together somehow, starting to lead somewhere. I just wasn't sure quite where yet. "Dear God," I prayed, as I drifted off into peaceful sleep, "Please help me to understand if You are really out there."

"Oh!" Penny's sudden gasp woke me out of a sound sleep several hours later.

"Penny?" I whispered into the dark.

"Did you hear that noise?" she quavered.

"What noise?" I asked.

"Shhhh!"

I listened. For a moment, all I could hear was Penny's breathing. Lady scuffled about down in the kitchen. Then the silence was torn by a shrill, wild howl from the depths of the wild, dark mountain night—a coyote! Outside, tied to her doghouse, Kayak answered back with a haunting cry. The coyote call came again and again, mingling with Kayak's howls in an eerie harmony. Lady gave a volley of fierce barks.

My scalp prickled and I shivered.

Chapter 19: Wild Things

"I hate that sound," Penny whispered fearfully, as the coyote howls rang through the dark night. "I wish they would stop."

I didn't feel the same way. Although the sound scared me, I could almost picture the red-brown coyote at the crest of dark hill, head thrown back, coat bathed in the silver moonlight as shadows played in and out among the wild rose bushes.

The howling kept up for a few more minutes, then gradually faded. Kayak and Lady quieted down and silence fell. When Penny's breathing assured me that she'd gone back to sleep, I rummaged quietly around for a scrap of paper and found Maria's envelope near the bed. Stealthily turning on my flashlight under the covers, I wrote as fast as I could, the words tumbling out of my heart.

Coyote Cry

Oh listen to the coyote cry,
The proud song of defiance.
The wolf-dog strains at her chain

Her voice rising to the sky.
Kayak, the wolf-dog,
The dog of noble blood.
Her song of love and mourning
Returns to the coyote
Alone on the hill.

I closed my eyes briefly, picturing the coyote silhouetted against the dark sky, and then put my pencil down. Within seconds I fell asleep again, and slept soundly until Penny woke me up the next morning.

"Hurry up, Jess!" My friend greeted the new day with her normal exuberance. "The sun is shining! Maybe we can go swimming before breakfast!"

"Uh, huh," I mumbled, hiding my head under my pillow. Penny tugged it away and socked me with it. With a groan, I crawled out of bed and looked for my jeans. "I don't think I want to swim right now."

"Why not? Oh, look, here comes Parka." Penny had curled up on the end of my bed, and was gazing out the window while she waited for me to dress. "She's got something in her mouth."

"What is it?" I joined my friend at the window, and together we watched the petite Siamese step daintily up the dirt driveway. Sure enough, she carried something small in her mouth, but she was too far away for us to see what it was at first. My little house cat seemed to have adapted well to forest life. She always brought home her treasures— some alive, some dead—to show the family.

"I think it's a mouse," I finally said, hesitantly. It looked too small to be a squirrel.

As the cat neared the wooden steps, she dropped her prey and paused to lick her creamy fur. Suddenly, before Parka could pick up the mouse again, something black dove off the roof and hurtled toward her—St. Peter! The crow landed a few feet away from the cat, and she looked at him, swishing her slender, black tail.

"She's going to attack him!" Penny wailed.

"Parka, no!" I thumped on the window, but neither creature looked up. St. Peter took a couple of perky steps closer to the cat, and she crouched suspiciously, tail switching back and forth, back and forth. I could just picture the lively crow dying in front of our eyes, but before we could do anything more, St. Peter hopped right up to the Siamese. To our amazement, he seized the dead mouse in his beak and flapped off into the air. Parka sprang after him, a second too late, and then stood gazing after the bird in astonishment.

Startled at this unexpected development, Penny and I gasped, then howled with laughter.

"Girls?" My mother poked her head into the bedroom, interrupting our merriment.

"Yes?"

"Is Penny ready to go? Dad and I need to take a quick trip into Torch Heights, but we can drive you home first."

"Oh, no, I'm not quite ready!" Penny started collecting her things. She'd come prepared for my birthday with at least two full backpacks. "I'll hurry!"

"Don't rush," Mom said. "We can wait a few minutes."

Penny didn't rush, and Mom and Dad ended up leaving before she was ready. Because the bear was still at large, Patrick drove us both up to Penny's house.

"Look at that box on the porch!" Penny said, as we stopped the truck in front of the cabin. "I wonder what's in it?"

As usual, she was in too much of a hurry to open the gate. She scrambled over the fence and ran to the house as Patrick and I came behind, lugging the heavy backpacks.

"A goat! A baby goat!" Penny's delighted shriek rang across the yard, and I ran to join her. "Look, Jess! A baby goat!"

Nestled on a bed of hay in the bottom of the huge cardboard box lay a small, brown goat, her long, gangly legs awkwardly folded underneath her. A white mark ran down the center of her face, and long, white ears flopped down on either side of her head. When she saw us, the little goat gave a weak "Baaaa!" and got clumsily to her feet.

"Is she for me?" Penny whispered. "Come here, little baby."

"She's yours." Hearing the noise, Mr. Ruffin joined us on the porch. "She's just a few days old, so you'll need to feed her with a bottle."

For the first time that I'd ever seen, Penny was almost speechless. She reached down into the box, gathered the little goat into her arms, and lifted her out onto the porch. The baby just stood there on shaky legs, looking around.

"What are you going to call her?" I asked eagerly.

"Hmmm…" Penny thought a moment, then smiled as if the perfect name had suddenly occurred to her. "Dorcas."

"Dorcas?" all three of us echoed in surprise. I must admit I'd been thinking more of "Nanny" or "Nibble" or "Ragtag."

"Yeah, like the lady that Peter raised from the dead in the Bible." That solved, Penny turned practically to other matters. "Daddy, is it time to feed her yet?"

"Sure is." Mr. Ruffin produced a glass bottle of warm milk formula, fastened a black rubber nipple on the top, and showed us how to coax the bottle into the little goat's mouth. It took several tries, but finally the kid caught on and sucked greedily. As she nursed, she gradually dropped to her front knees, and kept on sucking with her little back end sticking up in the air. She hadn't quite finished when my brother finally pulled me away, anxious to get home before our parents returned.

As Patrick negotiated the dusty, rutted road, our conversation turned to my new dogsled and my birthday. It was nice to just chat with my older brother. In spite of the fact that Patrick spent plenty of time teasing me, I usually felt comfortable talking to him about most important things—not *all*, but most.

"I'm glad that Mom didn't make me invite the Morrises to my party," I remarked. "It was more fun with just Penny."

"I thought you liked Dixie." Patrick sounded surprised. "She came to see you."

"Me? I thought maybe she wanted to see *you*," I teased.

Patrick groaned, but didn't give his opinion of our dark-haired neighbor. "I wondered. Well, anyway, why don't you like them?"

"They're just sort of—" I floundered for an explanation. "I guess it's Deanna that I don't like. She asked me why I believed in God."

"What did you tell her?"

I filled my brother in on the whole story. Patrick nodded, but didn't comment until I finished. Then he asked, "Why did that upset you?"

I frowned, hesitating to admit how much the question had shaken me, and remembering the minister on the radio who had talked about testing God. "She really made me wonder why I believe in God," I said finally. With a deep breath, I told him about the radio message.

"Is…was…well, is trying to find out if God is there, testing God?" I finished, rather miserably.

"No," Patrick said simply. "Testing God is asking Him to sin—like trying to force Him to do what *you* want, rather than what He knows is best."

"Oh," I said, pondering that new idea.

"Looking for proof isn't testing Him," Patrick added. "The Bible says that He wants us to seek and find Him, and Jesus even used miracles to prove that He was God."

"That's true," I conceded.

"But I think that once Jesus had proved that He was God, it was wrong for people to keep asking for *more* miracles," Patrick said. "They already had enough proof, but they weren't willing to accept what they had."

"Hmmm." I pondered that thought. It sounded like it really was okay for me to look for answers to my questions, but did I already have enough proof for me to believe in God?

Suddenly the truck gave a huge jolt and I flew forward, almost hitting my head on the high dashboard.

"Ouch!"

"Sorry!" my brother exclaimed. "Uh, oh."

"What?"

Patrick pulled the truck to the side of the road. As he shut the engine off, we could hear a loud hissing sound coming from the front of the vehicle.

"Oh, no," my brother moaned, opening his door. "I must have run over something."

We climbed out and stood in silence for a moment, watching the right front tire deflate. About thirty feet behind the truck we found a big pointed rock half-buried in the road and a piece of splintered board with a row of rusty nails sticking out.

Disgusted, Patrick kicked the board into the bushes. "I didn't even see it!"

"What'll we do?" I asked.

"Change the tire." Patrick looked into the truck bed. "There should be a spare here—oh, no, there isn't. Dad took it to Torch Heights to fix a leak."

"Can we drive home on the flat?" I asked.

My brother shook his head. "No, we'll leave the truck here, and come back when Dad gets home."

So, we shut the doors and walked off. It was less than a quarter of a mile, and we trudged along in silence.

After a few minutes, Patrick stopped in his tracks and tilted his head. "Listen!"

I stood still. The house was just out of sight, perhaps a hundred yards down the road, and the sound of howling came clearly to our ears.

"The dogs must hear us coming," I said.

"This sounds different," Patrick said. "Something's wrong."

Chapter 20: Don't Move!

At the tone of my brother's voice, a shiver ran up my backbone. I stopped in my tracks, straining to see through the trees.

"Come on!"

Patrick began to run, so I had no choice but to race after him. We rounded the corner of the road and the cabin came into view. Something *was* wrong. Kayak and Lady, both securely tied for once, lunged at the ends of their chains, deep growls intermingling with frantic howls. Kayak's fur stood straight up on the back of her neck. Then I saw Parka race up a nearby tree, her tail a huge brush of black fur.

I glanced around for the cause of the alarm. The clearing seemed peaceful enough.

Patrick stopped and I nearly crashed into him. "What is it?"

"I don't know." Patrick looked around, too.

"Look! The cabin door is open!" I stared. I knew I had closed it when we left to drive Penny home. "Someone's in the house!"

As visions of Dixie and Deanna danced in my head, I took a step toward the cabin. Patrick grabbed my arm. "Wait!"

In slow motion, the front door began to open, as though someone was pushing against it from inside. We stared in frozen fascination.

The dogs went berserk, lunging and growling. Kayak let out a strangled howl.

The cabin door crept farther open, and suddenly a black shape appeared in the entrance and lumbered across the porch.

"The bear!" I gasped.

The black bear hit the ground, moving across the yard and away from us toward Steller's Creek. I held my breath. Suddenly the animal paused. It half-rose, standing on its hind feet like a person with its forepaws held in front of it. I could see the white patch of fur on its chest as it turned toward us.

"Don't move, Jessica!" Patrick hissed through his teeth. "If you don't move, he won't see you!"

During that moment, everything seemed to move in slow motion. Bending slightly in our direction, the bear sniffed the air. For the first time, I noticed that the animal had a brown face, lighter than the dark black fur that covered the rest of its body. It also seemed thinner than I thought a bear should be.

"Just hold still, Jessica," my brother whispered again.

I'm not sure that I could have moved. I even had trouble opening my mouth enough to mutter, "What if it comes this way?"

"Then we'll climb that tree behind Kayak."

Out of the corner of my eye, I looked to see which tree my brother meant. There was a tall pine, but the branches were small and kind of high. I'd have to jump to reach the lower ones, but it was closer to us than any of the others.

The dogs still snarled and plunged at the ends of their lines. Turning its head, the bear observed them for a moment, then dropped back to the ground and meandered down to the creek.

I held my breath.

"That's right, keep going," Patrick muttered, encouraging the bear.

The animal paused at the creek bank for a moment. Then, plunging into the water, it waded calmly across and ambled into the trees on the other side.

"Ohhh." I put my hand over my face, my body sagging with relief.

"Let's get inside. Quick!" Patrick ran toward Lady, and unwound her chain from the tree. "Bring Kayak, too."

"Maybe we should go back to the truck," I said, hurrying to unfasten the angry wolf-dog.

She snarled in the direction that the bear had gone, and I held tightly to her collar. "No, you don't, Kayak."

"Mom and Dad wouldn't see us," my brother said. "And if the bear comes back, they might walk right into it."

"Oh!" I hadn't thought of that.

"We'll take the dogs in with us," Patrick said. "I don't think it will come in with the dogs in the house."

Cautiously we walked toward the cabin and stepped up onto the porch. Patrick peered into the kitchen window. "No more bears, but what a mess!"

We stepped into the kitchen. The house was a wreck. A pitcher of syrup had been knocked off the table and lay in two pieces on the floor. A huge, sticky puddle spread across the tabletop and the bear had tracked it all over the living room. Several chairs lay on their backs and a cupboard door swung lazily back and forth. A box of smashed eggs lay by the stove.

I shut the door, locked it, and stood shaking against it. "Oh, Patrick, what if we'd been in the house when the bear came?"

"We weren't," Patrick said firmly. "The Lord protected us."

"It wasn't even afraid of the dogs," I whispered.

Patrick leaned over the counter and ran his finger along the window. "Look, there's slobber marks all along here…on the outside!" I peered over his shoulder, and then Patrick swung around to face me.

"The bear came along the porch, looking in the window before he came in the door."

"What do you think he was looking for?"

"I don't know." My brother shrugged. "Us maybe."

"Looking for us?" My voice rose to a shriek.

Patrick hastily reminded me, "Who knows? But we're okay."

I shivered with a cold fear. "What'll we do?"

"Stay inside, I guess." Patrick stood by the living room window, gazing out at the yard. "The dogs will bark if it comes back. There's nowhere else to go really, until Mom and Dad get home."

"What'll we do if it comes inside again?"

Patrick thought a moment. "Climb into the loft and knock the ladder down," he finally concluded. "It can't get up there, and we can always open your window and yell when Mom and Dad pull in."

That thought was only slightly reassuring.

"It can't get in," Patrick added after a moment. "The door is bolted from the inside now. He'd have to break a window."

"Ummph."

We spent the next half hour cleaning up the mess. We heated a big pan of creek water on the cookstove and added plenty of soap to scrub with. I was in the middle of scrubbing the kitchen floor when I heard Patrick gasp. I looked up to see him staring out the window and pointing.

With a little scream, I jumped to my feet and ran toward my loft. I had almost reached the ladder when Patrick started laughing. I looked at him fiercely.

"Don't tease me!" I wailed, sinking into a chair and letting out a deep, shaky breath.

An hour later, Mom and Dad pulled into the driveway. As I ran out the door, I thought I'd never seen a more welcome sight than that old Toyota Corolla. Patrick was right behind me, Lady on her chain.

I threw my arms around my mother. "You'll never believe what happened!"

"What—"

"The bear came back!" I babbled. "He was in the house and—" Our story tumbled out, with many interruptions and exclamations from our parents.

Chapter 21: Day to Day, Night to Night

Needless to say, my parents were not at all happy with the news. My mother kept repeating, "Thank God you're safe. Thank You, Lord."

My father brought out a rifle and hung it near the door where the dogs couldn't knock it over.

"Should we shoot the bear if we see it?" I asked, wide-eyed. "If it tries to come in the house?"

Of course, I knew how to use the gun. We often hiked in bear country during our summer excursions, and my father had carefully instructed us in all the gun safety rules. We'd never actually had to use the weapon on any of our camping trips, though, and I'd never shot at anything other than a Coke can or milk jug, under my dad's supervision.

"If I'm here, I'll use it," Dad said. "If I'm not, then your mother. Then Patrick."

"So I just use it if I'm alone?"

"Go by the usual pecking order." My father grinned at me, and I knew that he was trying to get me to relax. "But don't worry. We won't leave you alone!"

He turned to my mother and brother, then, too. "I don't want anyone to shoot unless the bear is trying to get in the house, or is threatening one of us. We don't need a wounded bear on our hands."

After that, Dad and Patrick drove up to the Ruffins to warn them of the latest development. On the way home, they repaired the tire on the truck and parked it near the house.

Mom and I finished cleaning up the mess, and I decided to haul out my new webbing materials and get busy with Kayak's harness. Just as I headed toward the loft, though, my mother stopped me. "Can you help me with dinner? We told them to come around 6:00."

I stopped, puzzled. "Told who to come?"

Mom looked surprised. "I guess I forgot to tell you with all the excitement over the bear. The Morris girls are coming for supper."

"Whaaat?" I croaked.

"We saw the girls walking along the road and stopped to warn them about the bear again." Mom dumped the contents of a chocolate cake mix into a stainless steel bowl. "Dixie told us that their parents are out of town for a few days, so we invited them to eat with us tonight."

"For dinner?" I said in dismay.

Mom just looked at me. I bit my lip. "It's just they are so hard to get along with," I said. "Deanna said she doesn't believe in God. She said that homeschooling must be easy. She said..." My voice trailed off.

"I know they're not easy to have around," Mom sympathized. "But I think it's important to show them they're welcome here. You know it isn't an accident that they're neighbors. God must have a reason for that."

"I don't know what to do while they're here," I protested. "And I was going to work on my dog harness."

"We'll help entertain them," Mom promised. "Maybe they'd like to play a game or something."

"You'll play, too?"

"Of course," she said. "We all will."

Just then Dad and Patrick stomped into the house and helped themselves to the lemonade.

"When's dinner?" my ever-hungry brother asked.

"As soon as the girls get here," Mom told him.

"What girls?" Patrick sounded surprised. "Is Penny coming back?"

When he found out Mom's plan for all of us to entertain Dixie and Deanna, he protested long and loud.

"Dixie is always looking at me out of the corner of her eye and giving me silly smiles!"

"Maybe she likes you," I muttered.

"Well, I don't like *her*!"

"Listen, Patrick," Mom said, "We all agree they're not easy to get along with, but it isn't fair to leave this all up to Jessica. She's having to put her own plans aside tonight, too."

"Maybe they won't stay long," Patrick said.

"Maybe not," Dad said. "But we need to be welcoming while they're here."

Patrick and I both knew that. We all had welcomed people to our house many, many times when we lived in Kalispell. It seemed as if people dropped by all the time to visit or eat dinner with us. When I was little, Mom explained to me that having people to our house was like being a missionary in a foreign country.

"We can't go to another country," she told me. "So we need to love the people right where we are."

Anyway, inviting Dixie and Deanna for dinner was a typical thing for my parents to do. Usually, I liked having company, but not this time!

The Morrises arrived right at 6:00, and I welcomed them at the door. They appeared to be—well, themselves. Dixie had on red shorts, with a red-and-white striped top, while Deanna wore a similar green outfit. Dixie's fingernails, toenails, lipstick, earrings and bracelets all matched the red of her shorts, and she smelled violently of roses. Deanna either wore no perfume or the same kind as her sister. I couldn't tell.

"Hi!" Dixie said brightly. "Thanks for inviting us! It's so nice not to have to cook tonight!"

"Yeah, right," Deanna said. "As if you would cook anything, Dix. TV dinners hardly count!"

"Come in," I invited. "Would you like some lemonade?"

They did. As I hurried to pour the lemonade, Parka came purring up, and Dixie stooped to pet her. "Oh, here's that beautiful cat!" she exclaimed.

Parka arched her back with pleasure as Dixie scratched her along the backbone. "She's such a sweetheart," Dixie murmured. "Look, Deanna, isn't she pretty?"

"I suppose," Deanna agreed without enthusiasm.

At the tone of her voice, I realized that she didn't want to be here any more than I wanted her to be here. I wondered how Dixie managed to drag her along.

"So your parents took your older brother to school?" Mom interjected, setting our blue and white goose plates on the table.

"Well, sort of." Dixie stood up, cuddling Parka. "Derek's already been at college in Missoula for a year, but he's moving to a new apartment closer to campus. Mom wanted to help him move. And they had some other business to take care of, too."

"How does your brother like school there?"

"He likes it," Dixie said.

"He hates it," Deanna said at the same time. They looked at each other awkwardly.

"Well, he both likes it and hates it." Dixie tried to set the record straight. "He doesn't like classes much, but he likes his friends. He's doing fine in school, though."

"His friends are weird," Deanna said.

Dixie gave her an exasperated look and changed the subject. "Can we help with something?" She came over to the counter where I had started chopping up tomatoes for a green salad.

I looked around, but everything else seemed to be done. "I don't think so," I said. "I can finish these."

"Oh, what a pretty picture!" Dixie leaned forward to take a closer look at the little stained-glass suncatcher hanging in the kitchen window. It has dark mountains silhouetted against a red sunset, and beneath the mountains there's a verse from Psalm 19. My dad gave it to my mother as an anniversary gift years ago—sort of in memory of the summer she spent in a fire tower, the summer when they first met.

Dixie read aloud the words. "Day to day pours forth speech, And night to night reveals knowledge." She turned to my mother. "That's so beautiful!"

"What does it mean?" Deanna had come over to see, too. She sounded puzzled.

"Is it from a poem?" Dixie wanted to know.

"Well, as a matter of fact, yes," Mom said. "It's a Bible verse—a song actually—that describes how the beauty of the sky reminds us continually that there is a God Who created the world."

"That's interesting," Dixie said thoughtfully. Deanna remained quiet.

Day to day, night to night. In a sudden flash of insight, it occurred to me that perhaps part of the answers to my questions about God had been around me all the time. Could it be that the whole beautiful world that I lived in was "pouring forth speech" to me, just like the skies? Before I could think any further, Dad and Patrick came in.

In the hustle of getting everyone—except the dogs—to the table, the conversation changed to gardening. Dixie was trying to grow pansies in their yard, but she hadn't succeeded very well. Mom, an expert gardener (she once worked in a greenhouse, developing new varieties of roses), tried to give a few tips. So, the first part of our dinner went smoothly.

We were in the middle of our chicken noodle soup when I noticed Parka sitting by the stove, gazing quietly and intently at the dark gap under the kitchen counter. Puzzled, I tried to see what she was looking at, but couldn't see anything. Then I heard a faint scratching noise.

I turned my head and caught Patrick's eye.

"Do you hear that?" I asked.

Everyone else fell silent, listening. For a moment, I thought I'd imagined the noise. Then a rapping sound came from beneath the kitchen counter.

Thud! Thump! Thump! Thump!

As we all stared in frozen fascination, a skinny gray creature came scooting jerkily from under the counter and into the kitchen, dragging his furry tail behind him.

"It's the packrat!" I screamed.

Chapter 22: Worth It after All

"Look out!"

"Stand still! Be quiet!"

"Don't step on it!"

"Where'd it go?"

In our scramble to get away from the table and away from the rat, everyone shouted at once. Parka ran nimbly up the ladder to the lofts, and Cheeper screeched angrily from his birdcage. Outside, tied to the porch, the dogs howled with frustration.

When the pandemonium subsided, we discovered that the rat had disappeared somewhere—again.

"That packrat!" Dad said in frustration. "We've had the trap set all week! I guess I'll need to use a different bait."

Embarrassed, I looked at the Morrises, hoping they didn't think our house was dirty. My mother keeps things clean, clean, clean, but that didn't seem to deter our wild animal visitor at all.

"Oh, just an old rat." Deanna, who had screamed louder than anyone else, climbed down from the couch, trying to act cool and collected, as if a rat in the kitchen were no big deal.

We all returned to the table, with a few nervous glances at the counter, and Mom soon produced the dessert. Perhaps she hoped that the chocolate would have a calming effect! I don't know if her idea worked or not, but the cake tasted wonderful—thick chocolate frosting over deep brown cake. All we missed was ice-cream, but we couldn't keep that frozen without a freezer. Instead, we washed the dessert down with tall glasses of milk.

"What did you call it? A packrat?" Dixie asked. She'd been amazingly calm, and had actually tried to get a closer look at the creature while Deanna and I rushed past her into the other room. "Why is it called a packrat?"

"Well, it packs stuff," Patrick began explaining, and Dixie looked sincerely interested.

As they talked about wildlife, the conversation gradually changed to horses. Dixie could talk about horses forever, it seemed.

My father grew up on a farm in Idaho, so he knew a lot about horses, too. When Dixie found that out, she started asking questions about training horses. Somehow that led to a conversation about animal care in general. We found out that Dixie wanted to be a veterinarian. When she talked about the idea, her face just lit up and she even seemed to forget all about Patrick.

"Just to be able to work with so many different kinds of animals," she said eagerly. "I think being a vet in a zoo would be best of all."

"Do you have any schools that you're looking into?" Mom asked.

"I'm not sure yet," Dixie said. "I still have two more years of high school, but I'd like to work with a vet next summer, if I can. Right now, I help at the animal shelter a couple days a week, so that's neat. I exercise the dogs and clean cages—that part isn't so wonderful!" She grimaced. "But the nicest thing is seeing an animal get a home. I wish that would happen more often." Her voice sounded sad as she mentioned how many dogs and cats didn't get homes at all.

When the last of the chocolate cake disappeared, we cleared the table. True to her promise, Mom suggested a game.

"Sure." Patrick pleasantly took his cue.

"Sure." Dixie beamed. "What games do you have?"

"Have you ever played Dictionary?" I asked. That is our old standby. Even though we've got some board games and stuff, we always seem to come back to that.

Dixie and Deanna shook their heads.

"Oh, you have to try it," Mom said enthusiastically. (She loves to play Dictionary.) "We'll show you how. Jessica, why don't you explain?"

A few moments later we found ourselves seated around the table again. Mom lit the kerosene lamps so that we'd have more light. I passed out a piece of paper to each of us while Dad sharpened pencils. Patrick lugged our big, brown dictionary over and set it on the end of the oak table.

"It's like this," I started. "Patrick will pick a word from the dictionary that none of us have ever heard before. Then we each make up a definition for the word and write it on our papers. Patrick will write the real definition on his paper. Then he'll mix all the definitions up and read them to us. We try to guess which one is the right one. If you guess the right answer, you'll get three points. If your made-up definition fools people into thinking it's the right one, then you get two points for every person that guesses yours."

"Oh, okay," Dixie said. "I think I see."

"You'll catch on," Patrick assured them. "It's easy." He was already searching through the massive book for a word. "Has anyone ever heard of a kinglet?"

None of us had, not even my father, so we all bent over our papers. Pencils scratched busily for a moment. Then we handed our papers to Patrick, and he read aloud the definitions.

"Kinglet: the young of a kingfisher," he announced. "Definition number two: an unimportant king. Three: a crown worn by the Czar during the Golden Horde. Four: a baby kingfisher."

"There's two almost the same," I said. I wondered if Dixie and Deanna had been thinking along the same lines. A baby kingfisher didn't sound too unlikely. It actually sounded better than my definition about the crown. The "unimportant king" sounded too obvious.

"Number five," Patrick continued. "A puppet found in the tomb with King Tut. Number six: A royal ampersand."

At that one, my father chuckled.

"What's an ampersand?" I asked.

"It's an 'and' sign," my mother explained. "One that looks like this." She drew it on an extra sheet—"&"

Somehow, I suspected that was *her* definition!

"Okay," Patrick said. "What's everyone's guess?"

"The young of a kingfisher," I said uncertainly.

"I'll go with that one, too," Mom agreed.

"The crown," Dixie contributed.

"The puppet?" Deanna said.

"I'd have to say the young kingfisher, too," Dad said last.

"None of you got it!" Patrick sounded triumphant. "The real definition was the unimportant king. I get two points for picking the word."

"The unimportant king?" I said incredulously. "That sounds so fake."

"That's it!" Patrick said.

"Who suggested the young of the kingfisher?" Mom wanted to know.

"That was—" Patrick consulted the sheets. "Dixie. She gets six points because three of you guessed her definition. Jessica gets two points for her crown. Dad gets two points for the puppet."

We all got our papers back and started keeping score. "This is fun!" Dixie said. "What's the next one?"

"It's my turn." I appropriated the dictionary from my brother and started paging through it. "Just a minute. Has anyone heard of rigmarole?"

"Yes," Mom said. "Try another."

I prowled through the pages again. "Aha! How about a thyristor?"

"Yep," Dad said. "That has to do with voltage regulators."

"Threnody?"

No one knew what threnody meant, so pencils began scratching away. When I read the definitions aloud, I could hardly keep from laughing. "Threnody: a small Asian mouse; a song of lamentation; one of Shakespeare's heroines; a strange wooden box found in Egypt..."

The Asian mouse got the most points, to Deanna's delight. She added six to her score with that definition. Unfortunately, Mom guessed the right one—the song of lamentation—so I didn't get any points. Dad pulled in the rest of the score with his wooden box idea.

We played for about an hour, and it ended up being a lot of fun, laughing at each other's suggestions. Everyone grew more creative, and it started getting harder and harder to figure out the real definition. Dad almost always got points for his. Deanna, surprisingly, pulled a close second. I trailed behind, somewhere toward the end, along with Dixie.

We would probably have played for longer, but suddenly Dixie looked at her watch and gasped. "Deanna, we'd better go home."

"Aw," Deanna complained. "It's my turn to pick a word."

"Mom is supposed to call in fifteen minutes." Dixie jumped up for their jackets. "We need to be there, or she'll worry."

"Oh, did you get your telephone hooked up?" my mother asked.

"Yes!" Dixie smiled at her. "The phone company ran the lines last week. Are you going to get one up here?"

"Eventually," Dad said. "Probably next summer."

"Who won?" Deanna wasn't ready to give up yet.

"Dad did," I announced, after a quick check of the papers. "You're second."

"Oh, so close!" she groaned.

"This was fun," Dixie said warmly, towing Deanna out the door. "Thanks so much for inviting us."

"You're welcome," Mom said. "Come back again!"

"Keep an eye out for that bear," Dad warned.

"We will," Dixie said. "Definitely!"

I walked them to their Camry and waved goodbye as they pulled out of the driveway and across the bridge. They both waved back.

I felt warm inside. Somehow, giving up an evening of projects to entertain the Morrises suddenly seemed worth it after all.

Chapter 23: Free

"Hey, Dad?" Patrick's voice sounded muffled, as he poked his head underneath the big cream-and-green cookstove. "There's something in the box trap!"

"Is it the rat?" I asked eagerly, pausing as I stirred the pancake batter for breakfast. We hadn't seen the creature since the Morrises' visit a few days earlier.

"I think so—yes!"

I dropped my spoon and got down beside Patrick, trying to get my head under the stove, too. "Let me see!"

"Great!" Dad came out of his office and joined us beside the stove. "Here, let's pull the trap out. Watch out for your fingers! Let me do it."

We backed out of the way. Dad pulled cautiously, and the heavy metal box slid out from underneath the stove.

The rat, looking much smaller and less vicious than I remembered, hunched up in the bottom of the cage. His gray and black fur looked dull and matted, and his hind feet were a dirty white. He was smaller than my cat, perhaps nine inches long, and his furry tail was almost the same length as his body. I could see why Dad called him a "bushytail" woodrat.

The animal looked so helpless (and even kind of cute) that I felt a sudden stab of pity.

"What are you going to do with it?" I asked.

My father hesitated, looking at the miserable creature. Finally he said, "I think we'll take the trap out in the woods and let him go."

That seemed appropriate. Patrick and I jumped into the truck and rode with Dad toward the Lost Soul fire lookout. When we got far enough from home, Dad pulled the truck over to the side of the road at the base of a tall rockslide.

As Patrick and I watched, Dad slid the trap door open. Standing back, he nudged the rat through the mesh with a long stick. The creature hesitated a moment, then crept out the end of the box. Suddenly realizing that freedom lay before him, the rat sprang toward the bushes and vanished into the rocks at the bottom of the cliff.

"I'm glad we let him go," I said softly.

"I am, too," my brother agreed.

"Free to again terrorize the world!" Dad laughed. He tossed the cage into the back of the truck, and we drove home, anticipating Mom's yummy pancakes with warm huckleberry syrup.

An hour later, to our surprise, the Department of Fish and Game people pulled into our driveway in their pea-green truck. We were eating breakfast, so only Dad went outside to talk to them.

"They're hooking up the bear trap to the truck again," I reported, peering out the window.

"I wonder if they caught the bear somewhere else?" Patrick added more huckleberry syrup to his pancakes until his plate was a puddle of purple.

"I wanted to see it!"

"You didn't see enough already?" My brother raised his eyebrows.

"Patrick, do you want some pancakes with that syrup?" Mom teased, taking the pitcher from his hand. "Go easy on that stuff."

We munched in silence for a few minutes until the truck rumbled off, pulling the empty yellow trap. Then the cabin door opened and Dad came in, smiling.

"Well, they caught it." He sat down at the table again. "They trapped it down at that yellow farm that we always pass just before we turn up Steller's Creek Road. Apparently, it had been raiding there, too, so a second trap was set."

"Really?" I said, both relieved and disappointed. "What did they do with it?"

"They told me it was a young bear," Dad explained. "It had been in captivity before, and has a tag on it. It lost its mother as a cub, so someone fed it with a bottle until it was big enough to live on its own. That's why it wasn't afraid to come close to the house."

"Was it tame, then?" Mom passed him more pancakes.

"Not really tame," Dad said. "It could still have been dangerous. So, they tranquilized it and then set it free out in one of the wilderness areas where there won't be so many people. It hasn't ever actually hurt anyone, so they didn't want to kill it. It will probably adjust to living in the wild eventually."

"So they gave it another chance," I said.

He nodded. "They gave it another chance."

Surprisingly, I felt glad that the bear was free somewhere. "I wonder what it thought when it realized it was in a cage?" I said. I could almost picture it banging against the bars, frightened and angry. The bear wouldn't have understood that it had been trapped for a good reason-that it would actually be going to a safer place. The rat hadn't understood either, at least not until he reached the rocks beside the cliff. Now both creatures were free.

Patrick, apparently, had the same thought. "I guess we do the same thing sometimes," he mused. "Sometimes things happen that we can't understand. Later we might understand why, and see that it was for a good reason."

"Yes, life is often like that," Dad agreed. He leaned back in his chair and drank the last of his dark coffee. Mom handed him the coffeepot for a refill.

"It's a good thing that we can trust Someone bigger than we are," she said.

We all sat in silence for a moment, watching my brother finish up the last of the pancakes and almost all the syrup. Then Patrick and I cleared the table and got the Bibles out for our family Bible study.

We had recently begun reading through the book of Romans and sometimes I found it so hard to understand. It seemed to me that the Bible would be a lot easier to read if Peter had written more of it. Anyway, Peter didn't write as many books as Paul did, so we read Romans.

Today we reached the middle of the first chapter, and my father asked Patrick to read aloud. I followed along in my Bible, but got lost almost right away on verse twenty.

> For since the creation of the world His invisible attributes, His eternal power and divine nature, have been clearly seen, being understood through what has been made, so that they are without excuse.

My brother continued to the end of the chapter, but I just sat and frowned. What on earth did "attributes" mean? I thought it might have something to do with footnotes, because I'd written a research paper. I vaguely remembered my parents saying something about attributes. What did invisible attributes have to do with footnotes?

"Jessica," Dad said, turning to me. "Why don't you explain the passage?"

"Me?"

My father nodded, and I looked at the words again.

"Doesn't 'His' mean God?"

"Yes," Dad said, slowly and patiently.

I shook my head. "I don't know what attributes means," I admitted. "Is that for footnotes?"

My parents looked puzzled, but Patrick solved the dilemma. "That's *attribution*," he corrected. "Attribution means to give the correct reference to something."

"Oh."

"An attribute is a characteristic that belongs to someone." Dad stepped in. "For example, one of Kayak's attributes is that she's energetic."

"Or," Patrick put in helpfully. "One of Mom's attributes is that she likes geese."

We laughed, but I still frowned in confusion. "I really don't understand," I admitted. "How can attributes be seen?"

I stroked Parka, who lay near me cleaning her creamy fur. The cat purred softly at my touch and started licking my hand with her tiny, sandpaper-rough tongue.

Mom's face suddenly brightened, as though she had a sudden inspiration about how to explain something in a way that I would never forget. "It's like this," she said. "Remember when you found Penny's treehouse? You didn't know who owned it, but you came and told me that it was a girl's treehouse and that she liked birds. You had never even met Penny, but you figured those things out."

"Yeah," I said. What was she getting at?

"Well," Mom continued, "It's just like that when we go outside and look around at the world. We can see a little bit of what God is like (that's an attribute) by what He has created. We don't even have to see God Himself to know what He is like."

Things began to fall together in my mind. I felt my heart thumping, as if I were on the verge of a great discovery. Just as I leaned forward to ask another question, though, someone pounded loudly on the cabin door. Kayak, who had fallen asleep beside my chair, jumped up with a start and Lady gave a short woof. Dad leaned over and glanced out the window.

"Come in, Penny!" he called.

The door burst open to reveal a dismayed Penny. Her eyes were red and a few tears still slipped down her cheeks. "St. Peter is missing," she sobbed. "Have you seen him around?"

Chapter 24: The Builder of All Things

"Oh, no!" I jumped up to give my tearful friend a hug. "Oh, Penny!"

I knew how much she loved her merry pet crow. We all loved him. He couldn't be missing! He couldn't! "When did you last see him?"

"He hasn't been home since yesterday," Penny sobbed. "He always gets up when the sun comes up. Then he lands on my window and caws when I wake up. I'm afraid that something…ate…him."

"It wasn't us," Patrick reassured her, trying to be funny.

Penny managed a little grin. "I didn't think it was you!" she said. "Do bears eat crows?"

"No," Dad replied. "They don't."

"Oh!" I said. "Guess what? They caught the bear! And we caught the packrat, too!"

"Really?" Penny perked up a bit at this news.

I eagerly told her about the box trap and all that we knew about the bear. She seemed a little disappointed that we hadn't gotten to actually see it trapped. Like me, though, she welcomed the chance to walk in the woods again without worry.

"Can you help me look for St. Peter later?" she asked hopefully. "Maybe he just flew too far and doesn't know how to get back. Or he might be hurt."

I looked at my parents, and they nodded their permission. "If you take both dogs, and don't go far," Mom said.

We nodded.

"I have to go home now," Penny said. "Daddy's waiting for me outside, and he told me to come right back again. If you see St. Peter, will you tell me?"

"Of course we will," Mom told her. "We'll be praying for him, too."

"Thank you." Penny sniffed.

My father and I walked out to the Suburban with her so that Dad could tell Mr. Ruffin about the bear.

Penny's father looked relieved at the news. "That's great," he said. "A real weight off my mind."

"Jessica's going to help me look for St. Peter later," Penny announced.

Mr. Ruffin hesitated a moment. "Will you take the dogs, Jessica?"

My father answered for me. "We thought they'd be okay if they take both dogs. What do you think?"

Mr. Ruffin nodded slowly. "Yes, sounds good. This is the only bear we've seen around here since we've lived here. With the dogs along, they should be fine."

That solved, I promised to meet Penny at the treehouse later in the afternoon, and Dad and I returned to the cabin and picked up our Bibles.

"What were we talking about?" Dad asked.

"Attributes," Mom reminded him. "Romans 1:20."

"Oh, that's right." He looked back at the page.

"Is it like the verse from Psalm 19 on Mom's suncatcher?" I went back to Mom's explanation about seeing what God was like without actually seeing God Himself. "The heavens are telling of the glory of God...Day to day pours forth speech, And night to night reveals knowledge."

"That's exactly right," Dad said. "The sky, the sun, the clouds, the stars—they all show us something about God. What are some of the other things we can tell about Him?"

"I've got one," Patrick volunteered. (I think that he was just starting to understand, too.) "When we stopped by that waterfall on the way here, I thought about how strong and powerful God is to create something like that. That might help show the eternal power that the verse talks about."

I remembered the longing feeling that I'd had, watching the water roar over the rocks—the sense that something bigger than myself, bigger than any person on earth, must be in control.

"Nature shows us at least two things about God," Dad said. "Take a look at Hebrews 3:4."

I opened to the passage and read aloud, "For every house is built by someone, but the builder of all things is God."

"First, nature shows us that a Creator *exists*." Dad leaned back in his chair. "When you saw your dogsled for the first time, you knew someone built it—because you know from experience that everything is caused by something else. It's the same with the natural world around us—it had to come from somewhere, from some Creator."

I could see that.

"There's another thing that nature shows us." Dad, the theology professor, was warming up to the subject. "Romans 1 and Psalm 19 explain that nature shows us what God is *like*—that the beauty and design of the world indicate that Something intelligent created it."

"Here's another example," Mom contributed helpfully. "Imagine yourself walking through a field and finding an old watch, just ticking there all by itself. If you picked it up and looked at it, it would be complicated enough that you would suspect that someone, somewhere, made it. It didn't just happen by chance."

I laughed, recalling Penny's attempts to entice a packrat to leave her a watch that didn't belong to anyone. "Of course," I said. "Nobody would think that was just an accident!"

"Well, when we look at the world around us, we see a universe that is much more complicated than we can even understand. Doesn't it make sense that somewhere there is a Creator, a Designer, Who put things together for a reason?"

I nodded, my excitement growing. I remembered the little wood-burned designs on my dogsled—clearly Patrick's work. I thought about bright-eyed St. Peter and all the creative things he tried—the crow's ingenuity pointed to an even more creative Designer.

Parka, each clean hair smoothed into place, suddenly leaped into my lap. I marveled at her daintiness as she turned in a circle and lay down, trying to adjust to the confines of the chair. I thought about the awkward moose, the coyotes howling in the dark night, and about Kayak, my fearless wolf-dog. I saw nothing random in these creatures. They were more well-designed than anything that I could ever even imagine—designed by Someone much bigger than I, Someone incredibly creative.

It did make sense, a whole lot of sense. Somewhere deep inside me a great happiness began to stir. I felt almost as if I had started life all over again. With all the overwhelming evidence of God around me, how could I *not* believe? His whole creation seemed to be crying out to me.

"That's what is wrong with the theory of evolution, isn't it?" Patrick broke in. "That it doesn't explain the complicated design in the world?"

"That's one of *many* problems with evolution," Dad agreed. "But even if we were to believe that things do 'evolve' or change over time, it could just be a process that God uses—like you use tools in your shop. Your saws and hammers and nails don't jump off the workbench and start building without you."

We all laughed.

After the Bible study, I slipped outside into the sunshine and climbed the hill to my quiet spot, Kayak at my heels. Perched on the old, mossy log, I looked across the valley at the dark green and blue mountains on the other side, stretching away toward Canada.

Great clouds, in shades of gray and white, massed over the horizon, pushed by an unseen wind toward an unknown destination. The fresh breeze tossed the aspen leaves on the trees around me, and ruffled Kayak's black fur as she investigated a clump of creamy bear grass. Her narrow black tail, held low and straight behind her, moved almost imperceptibly as she sniffed.

A strange sensation, somewhere between peace and tears filled my heart. I suddenly understood the "knowing" that Mom talked about, backing up the reasons that my mind was just beginning to grasp.

"God?" I said aloud, looking up toward the sky. "Thank You for showing me the answer. I do believe. I do."

Nothing cataclysmic happened—but I guess I didn't need a sign from heaven. As Patrick explained, God had shown Himself to me and I didn't need *more* proof!

Overhead, a pair of dark ravens swooped and cawed to one another, almost dancing in the air, suddenly reminding me of my promise to help Penny look for St. Peter.

"Come on, Kayak!" I jumped to my feet. "We've got a job to do!"

Chapter 25: A Cry in the Woods

"There you are!" Penny popped up from her seat on the couch as I pushed open our cabin door. "Where were you?"

"I thought I was going to meet you at the treehouse," I said in surprise.

"Oh, Mama dropped me off on her way to work."

I exchanged my black leather sandals for sturdier tennis shoes, and Penny and I prepared for the big crow hunt. My mother kept adding things to our backpacks—matches (in case we got lost and had to build a fire), black garbage bags (to use for raincoats in case of a sudden storm), water bottles, sandwiches, a pocketknife…It was only with difficulty that I kept her from sending along a white sheet and a can of red spray paint in case we needed to signal a helicopter for help.

"Mom!" I finally exclaimed in exasperation, tucking a pink wool blanket into my pack. "We aren't going very far. And one of us can always run home for help. We'll be back long before it gets dark."

"Well, you need to be prepared," Mom began.

"We have my walkie-talkies, Mrs. James," Penny piped up. "Do you want to keep one here? We can call you as we go."

That relaxed my mother somewhat, and she agreed. When we tested the little radios, they worked fine and we promised to call home every hour.

Finally Penny and I reached the porch with our packs and the two dogs—and my mother.

"Keep the dogs with you," Mom warned, still reluctant to let us out of sight. "Do you have your whistles?"

Penny and I both nodded, holding up the yellow implements of battle that we wore around our necks. Penny blew into hers to demonstrate—a shrill screech that made Mom and I clap our hands over our ears.

"And I know how to use Morris code to signal for help," my friend added confidently.

"Morse code," I corrected automatically. "We won't go real far, Mom."

"We'll follow the creek toward the lookout." Penny slung her green backpack over her shoulder. "That way we can't get lost."

"That sounds like a good plan. Don't forget to call!" Mom still sounded nervous.

We waved goodbye and set off, walking as close to the gurgling stream as we could, with Kayak straining at her leash and Lady following close at our heels. Although the day was warm, the shady woods kept us a bit cooler and we soon discovered the one thing we had forgotten—mosquito repellent.

"These are awful!" Penny slapped her arm in frustration.

"Let's try walking *in* the water," I suggested, brushing in vain at another whining insect. "It's not very deep here."

Penny liked that idea. We waded out into the shallow stream, shoes and all, and began slogging our way against the current, trying to keep our footing on the slippery stones. The mosquitoes weren't much better once we entered the stream, and it took us a lot longer to walk through the water, but it felt nice and cool. Lady whined and ran anxiously along the bank, but Kayak followed me obediently, scooping up occasional mouthfuls to drink. Every little while, we stopped to call for the missing crow and slap at bugs.

"St. Peter!" Penny cupped her hands around her mouth and shouted as loudly as she could. "Come here, St. Peter!"

"Here, here, here!" My friend's plaintive cry echoed back from the cliffs, but we heard no answering cackles from the happy-go-lucky bird.

We'd walked for about fifteen minutes when my friend suddenly stopped in the middle of the stream. "Did you see that?"

"What?" I stopped, too, and Kayak bumped into my wet legs.

"I thought I saw somebody over there!" Penny pointed ahead, to the left of the creek. I strained to look through the undergrowth and thought I saw a flash of blue. Then, just as I caught sight of it, an agile figure scrambled over a log, away from us, and disappeared into the trees. Lady, on the right bank of the stream, barked twice and then looked at us. Kayak growled and tugged on her leash.

"It looked like a girl!" I exclaimed, as I struggled with my excited wolf-dog, trying to keep her from pulling me out of the water and into the trees.

"Hello?" Penny called tentatively.

No one answered, and nothing moved. We glanced at each other, puzzled and a little nervous. Who else would be in the woods?

"Hello!" I shouted.

Silence.

"Could it be Dixie or Deanna?" Penny scratched an angry red mosquito bite on her leg.

"I don't think they like to hike." I just couldn't picture either one of the Morris girls exploring along the creek. "And it's a couple of miles to their house from here. Why would she run away from us?"

"Maybe she's spying on us."

I shrugged, just as puzzled. I didn't know why they'd want to spy on us, but who else could it be?

"Is anybody there?" Penny's voice quavered.

No one answered. We stared hard at the place where the girl had vanished, but nothing else moved.

"Let's just go," I said finally. "Whoever it was must want to be left alone."

"Okay." Penny clapped her hands at another mosquito. "Maybe it was the guard from the fire lookout."

"Is the guard a woman?"

"I don't know. Last year she was."

We set off again, sometimes climbing out of the creek to skirt around large pools and deeper spots, and stopping often to call for St. Peter. We pulled out the walkie-talkie, too, calling home as we'd promised.

After a while we stopped to eat our "provisions" (as Penny referred to the big lunch/supper my mother had packed). We sat on a rock in the sunshine for a long time, drying off and watching the dogs explore. I let Kayak off her leash for a few minutes, but we watched her carefully. I didn't need another skunk discovery.

"It's getting kind of late," I commented, fiddling with the dial on the walkie-talkie.

"Yeah," Penny said, her head down on her knees. "I sure wish we'd find St. Peter."

"Yeah." I clicked the switch on the small radio. Nothing happened. Puzzled, I clicked it a couple more times. "The walkie-talkie isn't working!"

"Oh, no!" Penny took it from my hand and tried it herself. Then she flipped it over and looked at the back. "The batteries are gone! They must have fallen out somewhere."

"Oh, oh," I said. "We need to call Mom in a little while. I guess we'd better head home or she'll come looking for us."

"Yeah," Penny agreed sadly.

After packing up the remains of the lunch, we retraced our steps downstream, walking on the bank more often now because we were tired of being wet and we needed to hurry.

We'd only walked for five minutes or so when Penny suddenly stopped. "Shhhh!"

I stopped too, nearly bumping into her. "What?"

"Listen!"

I listened, but didn't hear anything.

"It's a crow!" Penny cupped her hands around her mouth. "St. Peter! Come here!"

We both listened again. Sitting by my feet, Kayak tipped her head, studying our faces curiously.

"I'm sure I heard him!" Penny's face was alight with hope. "Come on!"

She started through the trees, following the stream down, and stopping often to call the crow. Once I thought I heard him, too, and once we saw something black flapping away from us in the woods.

"I know that's him!" Penny exclaimed. "Come on!"

We pushed eagerly through the tangle of alders beside the stream, until Penny stopped short again. "Shhh!"

We both stopped, panting from our efforts, but the sound that we heard this time wasn't St. Peter's merry chuckling. It was a frightened human voice, coming faintly through the trees.

"Hello! Is anybody there?"

Penny gripped my arm. "What was that?"

"Is anyone there? Help me!" The voice cried again—a girl's voice.

Lady barked and ran back through the woods toward the water.

"Come on," I said. "Somebody's hurt!"

"Be careful," Penny quavered.

Together we pushed hastily through the trees. A moment later we emerged beside Steller's Creek again. In front of us, the clear water ran quietly over the brown stones, gradually forming a curve and disappearing around the bend. Penny and I looked around at the peaceful scene.

"Maybe it was just a raven?" Penny said doubtfully. "They imitate people sometimes."

I shook my head. "No, it wasn't a raven."

"Sometimes mountain lions sound like people," Penny whispered. "It might be a trap!"

In spite of the seriousness of the situation, I stifled a giggle. "Mountain lions *scream*," I said. "They don't yell for help! I heard one once, but this wasn't a mountain lion."

I had heard one of the huge cats scream years earlier, when my family camped near Glacier Park. It was an experience that I could never forget—a wild shriek that sounded like a dying woman. Just thinking about it made me shiver again with fear.

"Hello! Is anyone there?" The voice wailed again, much closer this time.

"Where are you?" I shouted back.

"Here! By the stream!"

Chapter 26: Danger in the River

At that last shout, Lady woofed and dodged toward a tree that lay across the creek, Kayak at her heels. Both dogs whined at the log, then worked their way around the end, crawling through the branches.

Just at that moment, Penny gasped. "Look! There's St. Peter!"

I jerked toward the direction that she pointed, just in time to see a small black shape swoop through the trees and out of sight, in the opposite direction of the one we were traveling. From that distance, I couldn't tell if it was St. Peter or a small raven.

"St. Peter!" Penny shrieked. "Oh, Jess! That was him! I know it!"

Well, we couldn't follow him now. Resolutely we turned our backs on the direction that the crow had flown and ran along the bank.

"Who's there? Where are you?" I called.

"Over here!" The voice replied faintly. "By the big tree!"

There was no doubt which tree the stranger meant. A huge pine lay half in and half out of the stream, forcing the water to whirl around and form a deep green pool on the upper side before it bubbled underneath the submerged branches. Penny and I had passed the spot earlier, walking carefully on the bank. We stayed out of the water this time, too, since it looked too deep and dangerous for wading.

Just past the tree, we saw a girl lying on the stony creek bank—a familiar girl with dripping brown hair, wet clothes, and a tear-stained face.

"Deanna!" Penny exclaimed.

"Oh!" our neighbor gasped. "You found me!"

The dogs had already reached her. Kayak sniffed her legs, while Lady settled herself beside Deanna's head and licked her face kindly.

"What's the matter?" I anxiously dropped down on the ground beside the girl.

"I think I sprained my ankle," Deanna whispered. "It hurts to move it, and I can't walk."

We looked at the ankle. It did seem to be swelling up some, and whenever Deanna moved, she winced with pain. Little drops of sweat stood out on her forehead, and she was breathing kind of light and fast.

"What did you do?" Penny asked.

"I crawled out on that log to put my feet in the water," Deanna said, tears in her huge eyes. "But I accidentally caught my ankle in the branches and fell in the pool. The current pushed me under the tree trunk under the water." She shuddered. "I thought I was going to drown, but I finally came up on this side. I think I sprained my ankle when I fell."

Deanna's face was tight with remembered fear, and she closed her eyes with a groan.

"She's fainted!" Penny gasped. "Quick, get some water!"

"I don't think water is what she needs," I said slowly, frantically trying to remember what to do. I'd taken a first aid class once, but all of a sudden my mind went blank. I breathed a quick prayer for help.

"I'm awake," Deanna muttered, shivering. "I don't faint."

"Quick, get the blanket out of my pack!" Suddenly my lessons on shock and fainting came flooding back into memory. Penny dug out the pink wool blanket that Mom had sent with us, and I laid it on the ground with my pack under one end. We helped Deanna to roll onto one side of the blanket, with her feet propped up on the pack, a little higher than her head. Then I pulled the other half of the blanket over her to keep her warm. Deanna whimpered with pain, but rolled into place carefully.

"You go for help!" I turned to Penny. "Take Lady with you." I thought it would be better if I stayed with Deanna, in case she really did faint. I grabbed Kayak and fastened her leash to a nearby bush.

"I'll hurry!" Penny sprang to her feet and set off immediately, running down along the bank of Steller's Creek with the Australian shepherd at her heels. Lady paused once, looking back at me, as if in doubt about whether she should stay or go.

"Lady, go home!" I commanded, pointing after Penny.

The gray dog whined anxiously, then turned to follow my friend. A second later, the pair vanished into the alders around the next bend.

I dunked my red sweatshirt in the creek, wrung out the extra water, and settled myself beside Deanna again, wiping her face with the cool, wet cloth. Suddenly I realized that my old feelings of anger had vanished. Instead, more than anything in the world, I just wanted Deanna to be all right.

"How are you feeling?" I asked.

"Terrible," Deanna mumbled. "But the cloth feels good. Thanks."

"I'm going to take your shoe off," I told her. "Just relax. You'll be okay."

Deanna groaned, but I tried to be as gentle as I could with the injured foot. The laces were tangled and tight, but finally the soggy, white tennis shoe came off. After wiping Deanna's face again, I put the cold, wet sweatshirt around her swollen ankle.

"How long will Penny be?" Deanna asked.

"I don't think we're too far from the house," I said. "Maybe twenty minutes through the woods."

"Oh." Deanna closed her eyes.

"How'd you get up here?" I asked, trying to keep her alert. She couldn't faint on me!

"I came through the woods," Deanna muttered. "Not up the road."

"Oh, it must have been you that we saw earlier!" I tried to sound bright and cheery. "We were wading up the stream, and we thought we saw somebody in the trees."

"Yeah, I saw you." She didn't explain why she'd run away.

We lapsed into silence. Deanna closed her eyes, and I saw a tear slip down her cheek. Remembering our first meeting, I wanted to tell her about what I'd learned, and how I now understood *why* I believed in God. If she hadn't challenged me with that question about faith, I would never have thought so deeply about it. I guess that her question was one of those things that "worked together for good" like the Bible said. I wondered how to talk to her about it, how to tell her the answers that I'd found. Was now the right time?

"Deanna?"

"Yeah?"

"Would you mind if I prayed for you?" I held my breath, anticipating a refusal.

Deanna looked surprised, then shook her head. "Go ahead if you want to."

I took a deep breath and closed my eyes. I must have prayed for a whole minute, thanking the Lord for helping Deanna to swim out of the treacherous hole, praying that her ankle would heal quickly, and that help would come soon.

"And thank You that we can know that You're with us," I prayed. "We can tell by the beautiful world You created. In Jesus' name, Amen."

"Amen," Deanna echoed, to my surprise. Then she looked at me. I didn't know what to expect, but all she said was, "Thanks, Jessica." She closed her eyes again.

I kept on talking, asking her questions, and trying to keep her awake. I told her how the packrat had been trapped, and what Penny and I were looking for in the woods. I chatted about Psalm 19, the suncatcher, and what the verse meant to me. Sometimes Deanna seemed to listen. Other times, she just shut her eyes.

Finally, after what seemed like forever, I heard a crashing in the bushes. Lady burst out of the trees and raced along the creek bank. When she reached me, she whined and wagged her fluffy gray tail, anxiously licking my arm. Around her neck, someone had tied a red bandanna. I pulled it off her head and found a note pinned inside.

It read, "We're on our way. Mom has gone to get the Morrises. Dad."

I read the message to Deanna and she smiled. "I didn't know that Lady could carry notes!"

"Patrick taught her," I explained, rubbing Lady's ears. "Good dog!"

Ten minutes later my father and Patrick came into sight, striding along the creek bank toward us and carrying a folding cot. Soon after that, Penny came into view, leading my mother and Dixie and Mrs. Morris.

"Oh, Deanna!" Tears on her face, Dixie ran to her sister. "I'm so sorry I upset you! Are you okay?"

I wondered what Dixie had done, but never did find out. Everyone was in a commotion, trying to wrap up Deanna's ankle and roll her onto the cot so they could carry her out through the darkening forest. When we all finally reached our cabin, the Morrises hurried to get Deanna into the car and to the doctor.

Later that night, Mr. Morris (who had been away from home when the accident happened) came up to tell us that his daughter would be fine. She had badly sprained her ankle (not broken it), and she was already home. He thanked Penny and me for getting help.

"There's no telling how long she'd have been there if you girls hadn't come along," he said. "She would have had a hard time making it home on that ankle. We didn't know where she was, and it would have taken hours for us to find her."

I wondered again what Deanna was doing out in the woods so far from her house—and without telling her parents where she'd gone! Quietly, I thanked the Lord that Penny and I found her at the right time.

"I'm so glad she's all right," Penny whispered to me as Mr. Morris's car pulled out of the driveway. "I was afraid she would die before I could get help!"

I thought of my anxious wait beside the river and nodded in agreement. It was only after Penny and her father gathered up their things and headed for home that I remembered—we still hadn't found St. Peter.

Chapter 27: Even in Here

When I woke up the next day, my first thoughts were of Deanna and then of Penny's crow. Had we really seen St. Peter in the woods the day before? I remembered the determination on Penny's face as she turned to help Deanna, rather than following after the bird. She'd never even mentioned our search again. Perhaps we could look again this afternoon. We had to!

After dressing quickly, I ran a brush through my hair and climbed down the ladder into the kitchen. Lady greeted me with a wagging tail, so I stopped to pet her for a moment. She talked to me with soft groaning noises. Outside, Kayak's claws clicked across the porch, and I wondered how she'd gotten untied.

Everyone else still slept. This was so unusual that I decided to make breakfast as a surprise. I puttered happily around in the kitchen for half an hour, mixing up a coffee cake. I couldn't bake it until someone started a fire, so I waited quietly for a long time before deciding to start one myself. I'd often built campfires, although I'd never tried to build a fire in a wood stove. The wood box had been well-stocked with kindling and firewood, so I didn't need to chop any.

Cautiously, I opened the little door in the front of the cookstove and looked in. There weren't too many ashes, so I just placed several sheets of crumpled paper in there, with tiny sticks of wood on top. Then I took a match, lit the paper, and closed the door. After a moment, to my horror, smoke started curling up through the stovetop into the kitchen. I opened the ash door again, and a whole cloud billowed into the room. My eyes stung from the smoke and filled with tears. I shoved the door closed and fanned the smoke. It didn't do any good. More and more little gray tongues whisked up through the cracks on the black metal stovetop. I coughed.

It only took a moment for the entire house to fill with smoke, and sounds of alarm soon came from my parents' room.

"Patrick? Are you building a fire?" Dad called.

"It's just me," I called back. "I was trying to build a fire, but I can't get it to stop smoking!"

Dad came hastily and sleepily into the kitchen.

"You didn't open the draft," he choked.

He turned a handle on the stovepipe, and adjusted another handle on the side of the cookstove. Almost immediately, smoke stopped rolling into the room, and a dull roaring noise came from the firebox as the flames really took off. Dad added more wood.

"You always need to open the drafts when you start a fire," he explained. "It needs oxygen to burn—that's why the air goes in from the side. Then the smoke has to be able to go up the chimney—that's why you open the stovepipe."

"Oh," I said, embarrassed.

Mom came into the kitchen, fastening her yellow bathrobe. She opened the front door, letting Lady and the smoke out. Seizing her chance, Kayak trotted in. She detoured past the garbage can and sniffed around the kitchen.

"What are you making?" Mom pushed the coffeepot onto the slightly warm stovetop.

"Breakfast," I explained, rather lamely. "I thought I'd bake a coffee cake."

"What a nice idea! That sounds wonderful." She yawned again.

"Building a fire will get easier," Dad said. "Once you catch on."

The coffee cake turned out amazingly well, after my bad beginning, and both my parents seemed pleased that I'd made the effort. Patrick, who polished off nearly half of it, was encouraging, too. "You should do this every day," he suggested, scraping the last of the crumbs from the pan.

We had just cleared the table when someone banged on the door. Patrick opened it, and Penny tumbled in, her hair flying. "St. Peter's come home!" she gasped.

"Really?" I jumped up eagerly.

"Oh, Penny, that's wonderful!" Mom said.

"He just flew in." My friend flopped onto the couch. "And he ate and ate and ate. He was starving!"

"Where is he?" I wanted to know.

"In the house," Penny said. "I locked him in the kitchen so he couldn't get away again."

"In the kitchen?" Mom hid a bit of a smile. "Aren't your parents home?"

"No." Penny shook her head. "Dad took Mom to work. He'll be back soon."

"What will your mother think about a crow loose in her kitchen?" Mom asked.

"I don't think she'll mind," Penny said doubtfully. "I don't think…Can Jessica come home with me?"

Permission granted, I left my family at the table and raced outside with Penny. I swung onto my red bike, and side-by-side we peddled furiously out the drive and up the dusty road. Huge, yellow-winged grasshoppers whirred out of our way, and I kept my mouth shut to avoid inhaling anything. I had once swallowed a fly or something, and I do try to learn from experience.

We tore into Penny's yard, dropped our bikes beside the porch, and raced into the kitchen. Sure enough, the crow was perched on the sink, looking at us with bright black eyes. Our sudden entrance startled him, and he flew up with a caw and tried to settle on the lamp hanging over the table. It took a moment for him to get his footing on the slippery metal.

"Come here, St. Peter," Penny coaxed, producing a little piece of bread from her pocket.

"Ha! Ha! Ha!" laughed the bird.

I laughed, too, unable to resist.

"Maybe we'd better take him outside," Penny said doubtfully. "I'll climb on the table and try to catch him."

This she did, stepping cautiously over the centerpiece—a bouquet of dried wild flowers and a fat yellow candle. No sooner had Penny gotten her balance when St. Peter flew down and landed on my head. I shrieked in surprise, feeling his little feet in my hair.

"Hold still!" Penny hollered. "And be really quiet!"

I tried, but by the time she clambered down, the crow had flapped to the shiny counter. Penny stepped gently toward the bird, the bread in her outstretched hand. St. Peter preened his feathers a bit, glanced at the bread with a bright eye, then decisively hopped over and took it—as though he'd never had any intention of doing otherwise. Penny gently picked him up, and the bird marched up her arm and stood on her shoulder, gently nibbling her ear.

"Ouch!" Penny said. "Now what should I do with you?"

Just then the solution to the problem arrived—Penny's father, back from taking Mrs. Ruffin to work. He took in the situation as Penny poured out the story.

"Well," he said after a moment, "We can't keep him caged up; he'd only be unhappy. I think the best thing to do is to let him keep flying outside."

"But what if he flies away?" Penny wailed.

"He'll probably keep hanging around," Mr. Ruffin said. "At least for awhile anyway. Eventually he may grow wilder and fly away, but we can't keep him caged, Honey. He's a wild creature, and he'd only be unhappy."

"I know," Penny admitted sadly. "He couldn't fly in a cage, and he's so happy flying. When I had penned him up, he just flapped around and tried to get out."

Her father put an arm around her. "He's an adventurer and he likes to explore! If you keep feeding him, though, he may hang around for awhile yet."

Penny carefully carried St. Peter outside. He flapped his shiny black wings and flew up into a tall pine tree. When we walked away, he swooped down low over our heads and let out a happy cackle, dragging his crow-feet through Penny's hair. We both laughed.

"I need to go home for our Bible study," I said. "Mom said to only stay an hour. Do you want to visit Deanna tomorrow?"

"Sure," Penny agreed.

We planned to meet the next day at two o'clock, so I set off, walking my bicycle.

The dust came up in little puffs around my feet as I moved slowly, enjoying the sunshine and slight breeze, and rejoicing in the beautiful world around me. Overhead, three graceful Canada geese called to each other as they passed over the trees. "Ka-ronk! Ka-ronk!"

A deep sense of joy stayed with me all day, as I helped Mom with some canning, cleaned the kerosene lamps, and worked on my blue dog harness. Later, when I went to bed, I couldn't sleep right away. Sitting up, I put my elbows on the windowsill, pushed aside the bit of white curtain, and looked out at the dark forest.

Overhead, a full moon shone a silvery light over the mountains, and the millions of stars seemed close enough to reach out and touch. The emotion of the past few days welled up inside me again, and I turned on my flashlight and pulled out a little notebook and pencil. The words seemed to flow onto the paper.

The Heavens Declare

I open my curtains and gaze at the sky,
At the moon and the stars shining on high
The heavens declare His handiwork.

I close my curtains, close out the night;
I'm shut in my room, shut in with my light.
I feel His presence, even in here;
I know with assurance that my God is near.

Laying aside my pencil, I cuddled back under my pink-and-white quilt, thinking about the eventful summer and wondering what winter would be like at Steller's Creek. Could we ice-skate on the river? Would Kayak learn to pull my new dogsled? What could Penny and I do outside together in the cold? I wondered if Dixie and Deanna would like to join us for a bonfire and sledding some moonlit night.

When that thought crossed my mind, I smiled.

THE END

Afterword:
What Jessica Discovered

During Jessica's search for God, she discovered some important truths. Although no one can measure and experiment on God (as scientists can measure and experiment with nature), many people believe that there is plenty of evidence for God's existence.

Theists are people who believe in the existence of a God. In addition, they believe that human beings can know certain facts about what God is like. Throughout history, theists have organized their evidence in the form of "arguments." An "argument," used in this way, is not a verbal battle. It is a set of statements that lead to a logical conclusion.

Through the centuries, theologians and philosophers have given these arguments names. Here is a brief summary of the three arguments that Jessica discovered.

1. The Cosmological Argument suggests that the existence of the world shows us that God *exists*. "Cosmo" is from a Greek word that means world. Basically, this argument points out that everything is caused by something else. By observing the natural world, we conclude that someone—a Creator—must have caused it at some point in history. The Cosmological Argument is sometimes called the First Cause Argument.

When Jessica saw her dogsled for the first time, she knew that someone had to build it.

Hebrews 3:4 tells us, "For every house is built by someone, but the builder of all things is God."

2. The Teleological Argument suggests that the design of nature shows us what this Creator must be *like*. It suggests that the complexity and beauty of nature show us that God must be intelligent and interested in beauty and design. This argument is sometimes called the Argument from Design.

Romans 1:20 reminds us, "For since the creation of the world His invisible attributes, His eternal power and divine nature, have been clearly seen, being understood through what has been made..." (See also Psalm 19.)

One version of this argument, written by William Paley, is called Paley's Watchmaker Argument. He suggests that if a man were crossing a field and found a watch, that man would conclude that the watch must have a maker who designed it for a purpose—measuring time.

When Jessica discovered the treehouse, she rightly concluded that the owner must be a girl who liked birds. She could tell by the furnishings of the treehouse. When she looked at the wood-burned figures on her dogsled, she could tell that Patrick had done the work.

While nature tells us much about what God is like, we also need to keep in mind that the world does not exist in the perfect state that God originally created. For example, God did not create the pain and sin and death that have destroyed so much (Romans 5:12). For this reason, Paul describes our current state as seeing "in a mirror dimly" (1 Corinthians 13:12). Because of this imperfect world, we must wait for heaven to better understand God's true nature.

3. The Argument from Religious Experience suggests that a personal experience with God is evidence for His existence. In this case, a religious experience occurs when someone sees, hears, or feels the presence

of God—as Jessica's mother described her experience in the chapel (Chapter 14).

A good Biblical example of this occurs in chapter 9 of Acts, as Saul is confronted by God on the road to Damascus. "Suddenly a light from heaven flashed around him; and he fell to the ground, and heard a voice saying to him, 'Saul, Saul, why are you persecuting Me?'" (Acts 9:3-4)

For many people, a religious experience of some kind is what leads them to God. Many of these experiences are real and true. However, since the Bible tells us that other supernatural beings exist (Satan, demons, angels), a person must be very careful not to base his or her entire understanding of God on such an experience. The Bible tells us that "even Satan disguises himself as an angel of light" (2 Corinthians 11:14), and that Christians must be careful what they believe (Galatians 1:8).

As Jessica's mother explained, she continued to read Scripture and learn more of God's truth. "All Scripture is inspired by God and profitable for teaching, for reproof, for correction, for training in righteousness..." (2 Timothy 3:16)

Things to Think About

Jessica needed to do some hard thinking to answer Deanna's question. She wanted to be able to "make a defense to everyone who asks you to give an account for the hope that is in you" (1 Peter 3:15). Here are a few questions for you to think about.

1. In Chapter 23, Jessica's father told her that an attribute is a characteristic that belongs to someone. Can you describe some of Penny's attributes? How about Lady's attributes? Take a sheet of paper and make

a list. What are some of God's attributes? (Hint: start with Job 34:21-22; Psalm 62:11-12 and 63:2; Psalm 147:5; 2 Peter 3:9; 1 John 1:9.)

2. While visiting Lystra, Paul told the crowds that God did not "leave Himself without a witness." Read Acts 14:15-17 and Matthew 5:44-45. How did God show Himself to these people?

3. Look at the following Scripture references. Which Argument do these verses remind you of?
- John 1:3: "All things came into being by Him."
- Acts 14:15: "God, who made the heaven and the earth and the sea, and all that is in them."
- 1 Corinthians 11:12: "All things originate from God."
- Ephesians 3:9: "God, who created all things."
- Colossians 1:16: "For by Him all things were created."
- 2 Peter 3:5: "By the word of God the heavens existed long ago and the earth was formed."

4. In chapter 5, Penny admitted that she'd never seen a packrat. She added, "But that doesn't mean there aren't any." Was she right? Did she ever see the packrat in Jessica's house? Did that mean that packrats did not exist? If we can't see God, does that prove that He is not real? (Keep in mind that no one has ever "seen" gravity. Scientists must rely on the *effects* of gravity to prove its existence.)

5. In chapter 15, Penny suggested that the packrat might leave Jessica a watch. What did Jessica say about this idea? Explain Paley's Watchmaker Argument in your own words.

6. Read Acts 7:55-56; 9:1-6; 10:1-23; 16:9-10. How did God reveal Himself to these men? How do these examples fit with the Arguments discussed in the Afterword?

7. In chapter 6, Jessica wondered if "faith was enough" to run her life. She felt that she needed more evidence to strengthen her faith. Why is it important to think carefully about what you believe? Consider Philippians 2:12; 2 Timothy 2:15; and 1 Peter 3:15.

8. What does God promise to those who seek the truth? Read Matthew. 7:7-11 and James 1:5.

9. Look at the following references. Why did Jesus rebuke the people in Matthew 11:21-24 and John 5:36-38? Read John 6:26-36. Do you think that these men were honestly seeking God? Or did they want something else?

10. What does Hebrews 11:6 tell us about those who truly seek God? What will God do for those people? (See also Romans 2:9-10.)

11. In Chapter 12, what made Jessica's father start searching for God? How does this fit with Romans 8:28? What other good things can come from our trials? (See Romans 5:3-6.) What were some of the good things that came from Jessica's struggles?

12. In chapter 23, both the packrat and the bear were set free. Do you think that these animals had repented of their actions? Or were they simply moved to a place where they couldn't hurt anyone?

13. When Jesus sets someone free from sin and death (Romans 8:1-2), what kind of change should occur in that person's life? Read Ephesians 5:8-10 and Galatians 5:22-24 before answering this question.

(For further references, see Philippians 2:1-5; Romans 6; Colossians 3:1-17; Ephesians 4:17-5:2; Titus 2:11-14.)

14. Think about Acts 17:24-28. God is not far from the people that He has created. In what ways did God "show" Himself to Jessica? In what ways has God revealed Himself to you?

Coming soon!

If you have enjoyed Jessica's story, keep your eyes open for

In the Shadow of the Mountains

By Anne Clay Cernyar

We slipped on our bathrobes, opened the creaky trailer door, and Deanna shone the flashlight tentatively into the darkness. The cabin lights were off. A few stars were visible overhead, but most were obscured by clouds. It was cold. I'd forgotten how chilly the mountain nights were, and I shivered.

We made our way cautiously toward the back of the house, with Deanna shining the flashlight from one side to the other and overhead.

"Why are you shining it in the trees?" I asked.

"Mountain lions."

"We've never seen a mountain lion here." Still, I looked up nervously. What would we do if we actually saw glowing cat eyes overhead?

We reached the outhouse without incident, and Deanna took the light inside with her. I stood in the dark, my eyes gradually adjusting. After a moment, to my alarm, I saw a shape I hadn't seen before—a lumpy, black bear shape. It looked like a cub, sitting on its haunches in the trees. Had it moved?

"Deanna!" I hissed. "Bring the light, quick!"

"What is is?" My sister was beside me in a second, and I swung the light in the direction of the strange shape. To my relief, it was nothing but the snowmobile, covered with a tarp. I exhaled with relief, and Deanna giggled nervously.

Our life in the mountains had begun.

***

When finances force her family to move to a lonely mountain cabin, fifteen-year-old Dixie determines to return "home" to her friends and private high school. A few things stand in her way, though—no money for tuition, no place to stay, no job, no driver's license, and a resentful younger sister. As Dixie tackles her problems, she makes some surprising discoveries about God, herself, her family and friends, and what really matters in life.

If you'd like to be notified when *In the Shadow of the Mountains* becomes available, send Anne a note at StellersCreek@juno.com or contact her through her author's webpage at iUniverse.com.

Would you like more copies of *Summer at Steller's Creek?*

You may order it

- through at your local bookstore.
- from an online bookstore.
- directly from the publisher at www. iUniverse.com. (Orders can be placed online or printed out for faxing or mailing.)
- toll-free by telephone at 1-877-823-9235.
- by mail from iUniverse using the form below. (Please call customer service at 1-877-823-9235 for the current price and postage.)

Mail to: iUniverse.com, Inc.
   5220 S. 16th Street
   Suite 200
   Lincoln, Nebraska 68512

☐ Yes! Send me_____copies of *Summer at Steller's Creek* by Anne Clay Cernyar, ISBN 0-595-13729-6, for the price of_____per copy plus applicable taxes and shipping and handling. (Please contact iUniverse at 1-877-823-9235 or www.iuniverse.com for the current prices before placing your order.)

Please charge my   ☐ Visa   ☐ Mastercard   ☐ Discover
                      ☐ American Express
Exact Name on Credit Card
Card #
Expiration Date
Signature

Shipping method

Name
Address
City/State/Zip
Country
Phone
E-mail

About the Author and Illustrators

Anne Clay Cernyar is a freelance writer who spent many of her growing-up years in Eureka, Montana just south of the Canadian border. Many of the events in this book have roots in her childhood.

She graduated from homeschool in 1990, and then spent several years tutoring other area homeschoolers before moving to Lynchburg, Virginia to study Communications/Journalism at Liberty University. She then worked as a writer/editor for The Rutherford Institute where founder John Whitehead described Anne as a person of "intelligence, integrity, and creativity" with "exceptional writing skills."

Since marrying Jeff Cernyar in 1998, she's published dozens of nonfiction articles, and enjoys writing about her interests—everything from searching for rare salamanders to negotiating the Mexican bus system.

Summer at Steller's Creek is her first novel.

***

John and Joan Clay, the illustrators and Anne's parents, lived in Montana for more than twenty years. Joan received her MFA from the University of Iowa. In addition to numerous short stories, she has illustrated two previous books, *Molly Helps Mother* (1994) and *Carmi of Judea* (1997) for Rod & Staff Publishers.

John worked as an illustrator for the US Navy and later received his MFA from Idaho State University. He is also a freelance artist who tutors privately and exhibits his paintings on request.